MOUSE'S SECRET CLUB
BOOKS 1-8

FUN SHORT STORIES FOR KIDS WHO LIKE MYSTERIES AND PRANKS

PJ RYAN

PJRYANBOOKS.COM

For my readers...
May these stories delight you.

CONTENTS

INTRODUCTION

Welcome!

I'm so glad that you've chosen this book of Mouse's Secret Club stories. I truly hope the child in your life will enjoy these characters as much as I do.

If you are just getting familiar with my books, please know that there are many series available, as well as some newly released journals that I absolutely loved creating.

Most of my series are available for Kindle, Audio and Paperback.

There are more stories, journals and puzzle books coming soon.

To get on my notification list (parents/guardians), be sure to sign up at my website. When you do so, I also have a FREE Rebekah - Girl Detective e-book for you.

PJRyanBooks.com

Happy Reading!

Sincerely,
    PJ Ryan

BOOK 1: LET IT SNOW! (INSIDE THE GYM!)

ONE

The whole town was buzzing. Everyone was getting ready for the new school year. First graders were hopping up and down waiting for the school bus. Crossing guards dotted the sidewalks and Mouse was grinning from ear to ear.

The first day of school was a very special day for Mouse. Not only did it mean a brand new school year to have a lot of fun, it would also be the first year that he would have his very own secret club. There wasn't much in life that could make him happier, except perhaps, a mouse in his front pocket. He peeked inside the pocket of his shirt to see a tiny white mouse peeking back out at him.

"Ready for school?" he asked the mouse happily.

Mickey wiggled his nose right back. As usual, the first day of school was about hurrying back and forth between classes and figuring out who had what teacher. The most important question, of course, who had lunch the same period? Luckily, he and his best friend Rebekah shared the same lunch period.

"Have you heard the news?" Rebekah asked cheerfully when they sat down together.

"What news?" Mouse asked.

"We have a new principal!" Rebekah grinned. Mouse looked at her for a moment, expecting her to follow up her announcement with an accusation. Maybe she would say that the new principal was smuggling diamonds, or that he was an alligator in disguise. Instead she just smiled.

"Okay," he laughed a little. "What's his name?"

"Mr. Davis," Rebekah said as she flipped open her detective's notebook. "He's from the next county over and he's worked as a principal for over ten years, and-"

"Is there anything you don't know about him?" Mouse grinned and shook his head.

"Maybe," Rebekah said thoughtfully. "But don't worry I'll find it all out!"

"I know you will," Mouse nodded with confidence. "Hey listen, I want to have a meeting today after school okay?"

"A meeting?" Rebekah asked. "What kind of meeting?" Then her eyes widened. "Oh you mean a secret meeting," she whispered loudly.

"Shh," Mouse warned her. "It's only a secret if no one else knows about it."

"Alright, I'll be there," Rebekah smiled. She was glad she was part of Mouse's Secret Club. Mouse spent the rest of his first day delivering messages to the other kids in his club. In math he passed Jaden a note folded up in the shape of a football. He read the invitation and gave Mouse a quick nod. In gym Mouse taped a note to a volleyball and bounced it in Amanda's direction. She caught it, read the note and sent the ball back with a smile and a nod. At recess Mouse caught up with Max at the water fountain.

"Meeting after school!" he announced to Max, who was in the middle of drinking. He spurted out water as he nodded.

TWO

After school Mouse headed straight to the tree house in the woods near the playground. He was the first to reach it and climbed up the ladder that hung along the tree trunk.

Once inside he pulled out an old dusty book that he had found there. It contained a variety of practical jokes and funny magic tricks. He had no idea who it, or the tree house had once belonged to, but he was glad he had found both. Soon the other kids were arriving. Once they were all assembled together in the club house, Mouse couldn't stop smiling.

"So, it's the first week of school," he began dramatically.

"First day," Rebekah corrected.

"Well actually the first day is over," Max began to point out.

"No, no, the first school day is over, but the first day of school lasts all day-"

"Oh stop it!" Amanda pleaded as she clapped her hands over her ears. Rebekah hid a smirk and high-fived Jaden behind Amanda's back.

"Okay, okay," Mouse burst out laughing. "What I'm trying to say is, this only happens once a year. I think we need to do something to make it special."

"The new principal Mr. Davis is having a special assembly at the end of the week to celebrate," Amanda informed them all. "The art club is helping to make posters for it."

"Perfect!" Mouse said gleefully. "I was thinking we can perform a magic trick for the whole school."

"You mean in front of the whole school?" Max asked nervously. "I don't know about that."

"Why not?" Rebekah shrugged slightly. "We know most of the kids, and those we don't we'll probably know by the end of the year. It could be fun. If you pick a good trick," she pointed out.

"Well I was thinking of," Mouse flipped through the book toward the back and pointed to the page that had a big snowflake on it. "Making it snow in September!"

"Is that even possible?" Jaden asked skeptically.

"Well it's all about the weather patterns," Max began to explain in a tone full of certainty.

"Not real snow," Mouse interrupted before they were all lectured. "That's the trick. We make everyone think it's snowing, but it's really not."

"Sounds like fun," Amanda shrugged. "Will there be glitter involved?" her eyes shined at the thought.

"No glitter," Rebekah said firmly. "That stuff gets everywhere."

"So it's decided," Mouse announced. "I'll talk to Mr. Davis tomorrow and see if he'll let us perform at the assembly."

THREE

At school the next day there were a lot of posters going up about the assembly. Most of them had plenty of glitter.

"Amanda's been here," Mouse muttered under his breath. The halls were crowded with kids still getting used to their schedule. When Mouse stepped into the principal's front office, the secretary behind the desk looked a little frazzled.

"Uh, hi, I was wondering if I could speak with Mr. Davis?" Mouse asked as politely as he could while trying to keep the mouse in his pocket from peeking out.

"Is it very important?" Mrs. Malloy asked with a frown. "He's very busy this week you know."

"It'll only take a minute," Mouse promised as he glanced toward Mr. Davis' door. "I can come back later if that's better."

"No, no, it'll be fine," she said with a sigh. "Better make it quick though, okay?"

"Absolutely," Mouse nodded. He knocked lightly on Mr. Davis' door.

"Come in," the man called out from inside. Mouse opened the door to find the oddest principal's office he had ever seen. Sure it was the same room it had been last year, but the furniture was very different. There were bean bag chairs as well as regular chairs. The curtains were bright and airy, and the window was open! Mr. Davis sat behind a desk that was made out of something that looked like Legos.

"Wow," Mouse said as he looked around. "I like what you've done with the place."

"Thanks," Mr. Davis grinned as he swiveled around in his chair. And by swiveled, he was actually spinning around in circles before he stopped to look at Mouse. "How can I help you?"

"Sir, I was hoping that we could put on a magic show at the welcome back assembly," Mouse explained with a wide smile.

"Well that sounds delightful," the principal said with a light nod. "I'm sure we can fit that in. Just make sure you dazzle us!" the principal grinned. Mouse really liked Mr. Davis. He seemed just as excited as the kids were to start the new school year.

"I'll make sure!" Mouse said with pride as he left the office.

FOUR

Amanda arranged with the art teacher to use the art room after school. Everyone in Mouse's Secret club gathered there when classes were finished for the day. Amanda set out the supplies they would need while Mouse went over the instructions for the trick again.

"So we'll each have our own cape and top hat," he pointed to the top hats and the shiny black material on the table. "We can just cut out our own capes."

"Oh you know what would look great on this black material?" Amanda asked as she picked up the material.

"Don't say it-" Jaden warned her.

"She's going to," Rebekah shrugged.

"No glitter!" Max insisted.

"Not even just a little sprinkle?" Amanda pleaded.

"Glitter gets everywhere," Mouse pointed out. "It might ruin our trick. We have to make sure everything is set up just perfect. Now let's poke some holes in these hats!"

They poked several small holes in the tops of the top hats. Once that was done, Mouse showed them the small fans that would fit underneath the tables.

"So what we'll do is use the small square tables and we can leave just enough space between them to set the hat on top. To hide the fans and the tables we'll use a table cloth, but we'll put holes in the table cloth too! We have to make sure that the tablecloth is taped down good so that it doesn't fly up and reveal our trick."

"I think you've thought of everything," Max said with a grin. "This is going to be great!"

"The assembly is in two days, so I want us all to make sure that we get to school early. We can't have anyone seeing us set up the table."

"Early?" Jaden groaned and shook his head. "Early and I do not get along very well."

"Just this once," Mouse laughed. "It'll be perfect!"

As he leaned over to stack the fans back into the box that he was hiding them in, the mouse in his front pocket slid right out. It landed on the art table.

"Uh, uh, uh," Amanda gasped as she backed up quickly. She was still not very used to Mouse's pets.

"It's okay I'll grab him," Mouse said quickly.

"Hurry before he gets into the-" Rebekah sighed and slapped her forehead. "Glitter!"

Sure enough the little white mouse had skidded right into a pile of leftover glitter. He was not white anymore. He was Mickey the glitter mouse, and he was spreading it everywhere he ran!

"Get him!" Max called out. "Don't let him get into the top hats!"

Jaden lunged for the mouse on one side of the table while Mouse tried to catch Mickey on the other side of the table. Amanda who had turned her back and covered her eyes was not helping at all. Rebekah couldn't stop giggling.

"Oh we need a picture of this," she laughed. "I've never seen such a cute mouse!"

Mouse finally scooped up Mickey on the other side of the table and reluctantly tucked him into the pocket of his shirt. He knew that his pocket would now be full of glitter, but that was better than a lost mouse.

"Remember, Friday morning everybody get here early," Mouse said firmly as he patted his pocket. They cleaned up the mess that Mickey had made and made sure that all of the items they would need for the magic trick were stored safely. As they were walking home from school that day Rebekah seemed to be excited about the trick.

"I think it's going to be fantastic," she said quickly. Mouse had never seen her so excited about one of his tricks.

"It has to be perfect," Mouse said nervously. "It's our first magic trick as a club."

"It'll be great," Rebekah smiled proudly at him, then waved as she reached her house.

FIVE

Mouse had trouble sleeping that night. He kept thinking about the trick and anything that could go wrong. He knew it was better to think it would go well, but his mind just kept drifting toward the worst.

Maybe the fans wouldn't turn on. Maybe the hats would blow up into the air. Maybe everyone would be able to tell that there were fans underneath the tablecloth. He tossed and turned in his bed, keeping his cage of mice awake as he did.

By the time he got up the next morning, he was very scared. He was sure that something would go wrong with the trick if he was not extra careful. He spent his day at school drawing diagrams and making lists of things he should review.

After school he sneaked back into the art room to do a dry run. He made sure that the fans were working and that the top hats were ready. Then he went through the speech he planned to deliver. Mouse had never spoken in front of a crowd before, and the idea made him a little nervous. So he set Mickey down on the table in front of him.

That way at least he would have someone watching him. As he went through his speech and then the magic words he would say over the hat, he was getting more and more excited. By tomorrow the entire school would be introduced to Mouse and his magician friends.

SIX

The morning of the assembly Mouse woke up extra early. He combed his blonde hair carefully. He even wore a tie. He folded up his black cape and tucked it into his book bag. Then he made sure he had everything he needed to perform the trick.

He even brought an extra box of soap flakes just in case something happened to the other boxes. He made sure he ate a healthy breakfast. Then he walked to Rebekah's house to meet her. Rebekah was yawning as she walked out of her front door. She hadn't taken as much care with her wardrobe, but he could see a black corner sticking out from her book bag, so she at least had her cape.

"I'm so excited," Mouse said happily as they walked toward the school.

"Are you sure that you're ready for this?" she asked him with a slight frown.

"Of course I am," Mouse said firmly. "I have my cape, I have my best tie on-"

"But don't you think you might be missing something?" Rebekah asked with a half-grin.

"What?" Mouse sighed as he stopped to look at his friend. "What could I possibly be missing?"

Rebekah lowered her eyes to the sidewalk beneath their feet. Her feet were covered in brand new green sneakers. Mouse's feet were, bare!

"Oh wow!" Mouse wiggled his toes a few times. "Guess I did forget something," he laughed and ran back into the house. When he came back out he had his shoes.

"Now I'm ready," he announced confidently.

"I hope so," Rebekah said with a grin. They got to school very early, not many other kids were there. Max arrived just after they did, with Amanda. Jaden showed up a few minutes later looking very sleepy.

"I'm here," he said grumpily.

"Okay let's get everything set up," Mouse said. They carried their supplies from the art room into the gym where the assembly would be held. The janitor helped them set up the square card tables. Then they placed each fan in the right place under the openings of the tables. Mouse made sure each one had a switch that could be pressed by one of the magician's feet. Then they worked together to spread the tablecloth across the tables and tape it down along the legs of the table and to the floor in front of the table.

"Let's test it," Mouse said. They each stepped on a switch and the fans turned on. The tablecloth rippled a little but it did not blow up in the air.

"Perfect!" Mouse said happily. They each positioned a top hat above the openings in the tables, over the holes in the tablecloth. As Mouse filled each hat with a good helping of soap flakes, Rebekah was staring hard at the tables.

"I don't know," Rebekah frowned and tapped her chin lightly. "I'm not sure that this will work," she shook her head as she peered closely at the fans. Mouse had them all set to blow on low when the switch was pushed, but Rebekah didn't think that would be strong enough. She didn't want Mouse's grand display to fail. So she just turned each of the knobs to high very quickly while Mouse's back was turned. As she was brushing back down the tablecloth, Amanda locked eyes with her.

"Rebekah, what did you just do?" she asked suspiciously.

Rebekah smiled innocently. "Just making sure everything's ready," she batted her eyes.

SEVEN

Amanda was still wary, but there was no time to ask more questions. The show was about to begin. All of the students had gathered on the bleachers. There was a lot of noise in the gym, with kids shouting and teachers begging for quiet.

Mr. Davis walked to the center of the gym where a microphone stand was set up. He tapped the microphone lightly with one fingertip causing a loud sound to echo through the gym.

"Welcome, welcome, welcome!" he announced happily. "Our first week has been amazing, and the rest of the year will be too. To show us a little of this magnificence, Mouse and his friends are going to put on a magic show for us! So let's all give them a round of applause!"

The kids on the bleachers all began to clap loudly. Mouse turned around to see the applause and couldn't help but smile. He hadn't always been the most popular kid in school, so it was nice to see everyone cheer. He just hoped that the magic trick would go smoothly.

Amanda, Mouse, Rebekah, Max, and Jaden took their spots behind the black top hats that were lined up on the table. Each one had a wand to match their flowing black capes. Even the tiny white mouse that poked its head up out of Mouse's pocket had a little scrap of black material tied around his neck.

"Since today is the first day of school, and summer is now behind us, we can start looking forward to our first snow days!" Mouse announced with glee as he waved his wand above his top hat. "So to give us a preview of winter, I and my fellow magicians will cause it to snow!"

A few of the kids on the bleachers clapped, but most groaned. No one believed that Mouse could make it snow at all, let alone inside of a gym. But Mouse didn't let their doubts stop him. He drew a deep breath and then waved his wand above the top hat before him.

"School is where we learn all that we know, now it will also be where it snows!" they all tapped their top hats at the same time, as quickly and loudly as they could to cover the sound of the fans switching on.

At first the trick worked perfectly. The soap flakes that looked so much like snow floated upward out of each of the hats. They drifted through the air with slow flutters. Then suddenly more and more came pouring out of the top hats. They shot high up into the air, much higher than Mouse had planned for.

"Oh no," he hissed through gritted teeth. "Something is going wrong!"

EIGHT

Rebekah was giggling in delight as the entire gym began to fill with the soap flakes. They were floating higher and higher toward the ceiling. The kids on the bleachers were clapping and cheering. Some were even standing up and whooping with approval. The trick was a big hit. Mr. Davis was laughing and cheering right along with the students and other teachers. The soap flakes swirled around the ceiling, and around the sprinklers.

"Uh oh," Jaden said quietly as he felt the first tell tale drip from a sprinkler strike his forehead.

"What is it?" Amanda asked peering up at the ceiling. She had a drop of water strike right above her eyebrow. "Ugh!" she reached up to wipe at her forehead and pulled away some bubbles.

"Oh no!" Max's eyes widened as he realized what was happening. "Mouse the sprinklers-" he started to say, but it was too late. The sprinklers burst on and began showering the gym, and all of the students and staff within it, with water. But the water from the sprinklers also mixed with the soap flakes still floating in the air. Bubbles were everywhere! The bubbles fell from the ceiling and bubbled up out of the top hats on the table.

"No, no, no!" Mouse groaned as he tried to cover his blond hair. "This was not supposed to happen!"

There were plenty of squeals as the teachers ran for cover. Most of the kids climbed down off of the bleachers to run out into the slippery gym.

"Stop, stop!" Mr. Davis shouted. He was trying to be heard over the din of the crowd. "Be careful! Don't fall!" he started to run toward the table where Mouse was standing with burning red cheeks. But his dress shoes slid in the bubbles that had collected on the floor. He went sailing across the gym!

"I am going to have detention for life!" Mouse yelped. Amanda and Jaden reached out to try to catch Mr. Davis but he sailed right past them. He looked very worried at first and then all of the sudden he started to make a very strange sound.

"Wheeee!" he cried out with a laugh. "Oh wow this is fun," he grinned as he began skating back across the gym to the other side. The students were as shocked as the teachers were as they watched their new principal have a great time in the bubbles.

The janitor had already turned the crank to turn off the sprinklers, but there were still plenty of bubbles spread around. Mouse knew that he wasn't out of the woods yet, but he figured he might as well join in on the fun. He began building sculptures out of the bubbles. Max, of course, sailed right through them. Jaden, Amanda, and Rebekah were having a soap ball fight with some other kids. Mouse peeked down at Mickey who was tucked into his shirt pocket. He had a little glob of bubbles on the top of his head.

"Well," Mouse said with a shrug. "Maybe it all went wrong, but at least it was fun!"

NINE

Mr. Davis let the kids play for a little while, before he bellowed over the laughing and shouting.

"Now that we're all soaked, please see Ms. Rose for your gym uniforms and proceed to your homerooms," he said sternly. Ms. Rose was out in the hallway with the large box of gym uniforms that were going to be handed out during assembly. At least all the kids had something to change into. As the kids started to walk out of the gym, Mr. Davis spoke up again.

"Not you Mouse, or your friends," he said quickly. Mouse braced himself. Mr. Davis had been having fun in the soap, but that doesn't mean he wasn't upset about the whole situation. When Mouse turned to face him, Mr. Davis had his arms crossed and his eyes narrowed.

"Did you plan this young man?" he asked Mouse sternly.

"No sir," Mouse shook his head quickly back and forth. "The fans weren't that strong when I tested them. I don't know how they got so high!"

Amanda shot Rebekah a look, which made Mouse's eyes widen.

"Well it doesn't matter now what went wrong," Mr. Davis said calmly. "You five have a lot of cleaning up to do."

The janitor walked in with mops, buckets, and towels.

Mouse looked at the soap covered gym. There was soap on the walls, soap on the bleachers, and even soap on the basketball hoops. He wasn't sure how they would ever get it all clean.

"Any magic tricks in the book that will help with this?" Max whispered in Mouse's ear as Mr. Davis walked away. Amanda sighed as she picked up a mop. Jaden began scooping up bubbles with one of the large buckets. Rebekah carried a big towel over to the bleachers to wipe them down. Max picked up one of the mops and swung it toward the basketball hoop, sweeping off the bubbles as he did. Mouse followed Rebekah. Rebekah was rubbing the bleachers clean when she heard Mouse behind her.

"So," he said as he pushed the mop along a puddle of water. "Just how do you think the fans got set on high?" he narrowed his eyes. Rebekah looked up at him innocently.

"Well I just thought that it would be more fun-" she started to say.

"Rebekah how could you?" Mouse demanded with frustration. "I had everything planned out perfectly."

"I'm sorry," Rebekah frowned. "I didn't think it would cause all of this."

"Of course you didn't," Mouse shrugged a little as he moved on to the next puddle.

"But Mouse you have to admit something," Rebekah said as she moved along the bleachers as well.

"What's that?" he asked without looking up from the puddle he was mopping up.

"It was more fun!" Rebekah laughed and threw a handful of soap bubbles at him.

Mouse laughed and threw one back. "Okay, it was!" he admitted. Soon all five of the kids were having another soap ball fight. By the time lunch came around they had the gym cleaned up. Ms. Rose handed them each a new gym uniform to change into. After changing, Mouse started to head for the cafeteria, but Mr. Davis caught him in the hallway.

"My office please," he pointed down the hall. Mouse winced. Only the first week of school and he was already being sent to the principal's office. Mr. Davis stepped into the gym to check on the clean-up while Mouse headed to his office.

TEN

Mouse pulled a bean bag chair up to the front of Mr. Davis' desk.
When the principal walked in, he looked pretty grim. He had
changed into a gym uniform since his suit was soaked with bubbles
and water. When he sat down behind his desk, he didn't look as
much like the principal, but his steady glare did. As he looked across
the desk at Mouse, Mouse tried to make himself as tiny as his name
declared.

"So that was quite an interesting event," the principal said
sternly.

"I'm sorry," Mouse said quickly. "I had no idea that was going to
happen-"

"Of course you didn't," the principal lowered his voice to a
whisper as he continued. "Tell you a secret, I didn't know that was
going to happen either!"

Mouse stared at him, feeling confused. He couldn't tell if Mr.
Davis was teasing him or if he was serious. "Actually, your little stunt
helped the school. The sprinkler system shouldn't have been trig-
gered by the soap flakes. If it wasn't for your magic show, we wouldn't
know the sensors needed upgrades." "Also," he sat back in his chair

and folded his hands across his stomach. "Our gym is now the cleanest gym the whole county!"

Mouse grinned at that. "Well that's true," he nodded quickly.

"But," Mr. Davis continued, making Mouse wince. "We still can't have these kinds of things happening in school. So I'm going to let this slide because I'm sure it will never happen again. Right?" he stared straight into Mouse's eyes.

"Oh of course, right," Mouse nodded as he was flooded with relief. He wasn't looking forward to explaining detention to his parents.

Mr. Davis nodded, making a note on the file in front of him, and then snapped it close. "Then off you go, back to learning!"

Mouse couldn't believe his luck as he hurried out of the principal's office. He was glad that Mr. Davis had such a good sense of humor.

ELEVEN

After school Mouse and the Secret Club met up at the tree house. Rebekah was waiting at the bottom of the ladder for him.

"So? What did he do to you?" she asked eagerly. "Is he going to make you scrub the bathrooms, or clean up after the football team?"

"No," Mouse laughed and shook his head. "He let me slide."

"What?" Rebekah said with surprise. "That's wonderful!"

"I think so," Mouse agreed. "Is everyone in the tree house?"

"Yup we were betting on whether you would survive," Rebekah grinned and climbed up the ladder. Once they were all gathered together inside the tree house they all began talking at once.

"The bubbles were great-" Jaden started to say.

"Did you see the look on their faces-" Amanda chimed in.

"I won't have to take a bath for a week-" Max laughed.

"I've never slid that fast!" Rebekah added.

"I can't wait to do it again," Mouse announced.

All the chatter died down at once. Mouse's friends looked at him in shock.

"What did you just say?" Rebekah asked, her eyes wide.

"I said I can't wait to do it again," Mouse grinned.

"Again?" Amanda frowned. "But don't you think we'll get in trouble?"

"We'll just have to keep our magical pranks, out of school," Mouse laughed. "And make sure no one adjusts the fans," he shot a knowing look at Rebekah. Rebekah whistled innocently and looked away.

Mouse pulled out a small scrap book from his book bag. "When I found this place I found a book of practical jokes, and I think we should have one of our own."

All of his friends agreed and they began documenting their surprise prank. As Mouse and his friends laughed and shouted, he was certain that this year was going to be the best school year ever.

BOOK 2: HAUNTED PLAYGROUND

ONE

Magic was in the air all over the small town that Mouse lived in. Actually, plastic bag ghosts, paper masks, and witch's brooms were in the air, hanging all over the houses in his neighborhood. Everyone was decorating for Halloween. Mouse always enjoyed this time of year because everyone liked a good scare. But usually he was the one dishing it out.

He was walking home about two weeks before Halloween, whistling a tune and swinging his book bag. It was a crisp fall afternoon and a quiet one at that. At least it was quiet until he heard the moaning and groaning from behind him. He quickly looked over his shoulder to discover a group of zombies slowly approaching him.

How did he know they were zombies? It had something to do with the outstretched arms, pales faces, and the drool. Definitely the drool. He ran as fast as he could to his house with those zombies chasing after him. Once he got there he locked his door and peeked out through the curtains.

He saw the zombies walking up his driveway. "No!" he shouted and went running for the bathroom. He grabbed some shampoo and a spray bottle. He mixed the shampoo and some water together inside of the spray bottle. When he looked out the window again the zombies were on his porch. He threw open his front door and sprayed wildly at the zombies.

"Back beasts!" he shrieked and the little mouse that was in his front pocket ducked down. "Back!" he shouted again and sprayed each of the zombies in the face. Their groans turned into whimpers as they wiped at their eyes. They smeared the white paint right off of their faces. As the white paint disappeared, he soon discovered that they were not zombies at all. They were the members of his secret club.

"Guys!" Mouse said with exasperation. "What were you thinking?" he ducked into the house and returned with some towels to wipe their eyes and faces.

"Rebekah," he said and handed her one of the towels. Her face was still streaked with paint and her green eyes were a little red from the shampoo. "Amanda," he said and handed the girl beside Rebekah a towel. She had closed her brown eyes tightly to keep out the shampoo but she still had some fake drool on her chin. "Max," Mouse sighed and handed him a towel so that he could remove the fake blood from the gash he had painted on his cheek.

"Sorry Mouse," Max said shyly as he took the towel.

"Mmhm," Mouse glowered and handed Jaden a towel as well. He couldn't stop laughing long enough to wipe off the paint.

"You should have seen your face!" he pointed at Mouse with a grin. "I wish I had a camera!"

"Ha, ha, very funny," Mouse sighed and shook his head. "We really have to work on your zombie groan Jaden. It was not convincing at all."

"It sent you running," Rebekah pointed out with a giggle. Mouse frowned and crossed his arms.

"Don't be mad," Amanda sighed as she looked at him. "We just wanted to surprise you and play a prank on you for once."

"Alright," Mouse laughed and shook his head. "I have to admit you got me."

Mouse's friends belonged to his secret club. In this secret club they plotted practical jokes and pranks mingled with some magic tricks. It was a lot of fun and they never ran out of ideas. But it was true that Mouse was usually in on the joke, and he didn't often get pranked himself.

"Where did you guys get all of the paint?" he asked curiously.

"Art club," Amanda said proudly. She was one of the best artists in their school and had free reign in the art room after school. Usually this meant that everything was covered in glitter.

"Are you guys ready for Halloween?" Mouse asked as he gathered up all of the paint covered towels.

"I guess," Max said with a frown.

"What's wrong?" Mouse asked.

"Well Halloween is a lot of pressure you know. We have to think of something great to do!" Max announced all at once.

"Something better than zombies," Jaden agreed.

"Something so spooky no one will be able to sleep at night!" Amanda added with glee. Everyone looked at her with slightly horrified stares. "Okay okay, just not for one night," she smiled innocently.

TWO

After school the next day they gathered at the playground. At the edge of the grassy field they each sneaked into the woods. Not too far into the woods was where they held their secret meetings. Mouse's clubhouse was a tree house that had a rope ladder dangling from it. None of them knew who had built the tree house, Mouse had just found it one day. Now it belonged to them, along with the book of magic tricks and pranks they found inside.

One by one they climbed the rope ladder as quietly as they could. It was important not to make too much noise. They didn't want other kids on the playground to know that the tree house was there. Mouse had posted signs for other kids to keep out. Once inside they gathered close around the book of pranks and tricks.

"So what are we going to do?" Max asked as he looked over the ideas in the book.

"It has to be something great!" Amanda announced. "Something spectacularly spooky!"

"Oh clever," Rebekah giggled and so did Jaden.

"Don't you mean Spook-tacular?" he laughed.

"Good one," Max grinned and then shook his head. "But we still didn't pick a prank."

"I know," Mouse said and lowered his voice. "It has to be something really scary. Maybe like a haunted house!"

"No way," Jaden groaned. "Everyone does a haunted house around Halloween. We can't do that. We have to do something surprising, different, something no one expects!"

"Hm, where would people expect to be scared the least?" Rebekah said thoughtfully. She loved a good puzzle to figure out.

"The grocery store," Amanda suggested.

"Ehh," Mouse shook his head. "Too messy."

"The library?" Max snapped his fingers and smiled.

"Ehh," Mouse shook his head. "Too quiet. We'd be kicked out before we could even set up."

"The beach," Jaden said with confidence.

"Uh, have you never heard of sharks?" Rebekah asked with a frown.

"Good point," Jaden laughed. "I guess the beach can be a scary place."

"But an outside place would be good," Mouse said as he rubbed his chin. Just then they heard some playful shrieks come from the nearby playground. The screams were loud but they were full of laughter, not fear.

"That's it," Mouse said with a dark smirk. "The playground!"

"Oh that's perfect," Rebekah agreed and clapped her hands.

"I don't know," Amanda frowned. "Don't you think some things are just not to be toyed with?"

"Nope, sorry," Mouse shook his head firmly. "The playground is fair game. I think it's time we gave kids a reason to think twice about getting on the swings."

"I love it," Max nodded.

"But why would anyone go to a haunted playground?" Jaden pointed out.

"They won't know it's haunted," Mouse replied. "We'll spread rumors about scary things happening. Then only the kids brave enough to check it out will be the ones that get spooked!"

"Not a bad idea," Amanda finally agreed.

"What kind of rumors are we going to spread?" Jaden asked curiously.

"Well we can't all spread them," Mouse said firmly. "Or people will get suspicious. Let's see," he pointed at Max. "I want you and..." he pointed at Amanda. "...you to be the ones to spread the rumors. Just make up some ghost stories. It'll be great!" Mouse rubbed his hands together with glee.

THREE

The next day at school Amanda and Max fulfilled their promise. Amanda told all of her friends about the scary experience she had at the playground.

"I stayed a little longer than I should have," she admitted in a whisper. "Usually I head home right before sunset. But I was having so much fun shooting hoops, I decided to stay a little longer. By the time I was done all of the other kids were gone. The playground was empty and I was alone," she sighed dramatically. Her friends that she was sitting with at lunch drew closer to her, eager to hear what happened next. "I started walking down the sidewalk to leave the park, but then I heard these strange noises. Like moans," she shivered in fear. "I thought someone might be in trouble or hurt so I looked around to see where they were coming from."

"What did you see?" a girl sitting across from her asked, her eyes wide.

"Faces floating in the air!" Amanda announced. "Vampires, werewolves, monsters, all of them!"

"Oh no!" another girl shrieked beside her. "Did you run?"

"I tried to, but," she closed her eyes tightly as if she was terrified.

"When I turned to run there was a ghost right in front of me! Then I heard all of this clanging and rattling!"

"Wow," a boy on the other side of her shook his head. "I would have been screaming for help."

"I was so scared that I couldn't scream," Amanda sighed. "I closed my eyes and ran as fast as I could. I didn't think I was going to make it off the playground."

"That sounds like a made up story to me," another boy said skeptically. "Why would all of those monsters be together at the playground?"

"I don't know," Amanda shook her head. "Maybe monsters like playgrounds too."

FOUR

Max was playing tag in the gym with the other kids in his class. When one of the kids reached out to tag him, he shrieked.

"Oh no it's happening again!" he cried out and ran as fast as he could. Just as he had hoped, all of the kids wanted to know what was wrong. Max really played the part of gasping, his eyes huge with fear.

"I'm sorry guys, I know we're just playing a game, but I recently had something really scary happen to me at the playground."

"What could be scary at the playground?" one of his friends laughed.

"Nothing," Max shrugged a little. "In the day time."

"Were you there after dark?" a girl asked as she sat down beside him on the floor.

"Yes," Max nodded. "Biggest mistake I ever made. I thought I had forgotten my football there. So I went back after dinner. It was really dark, and no one else was there. I started walking across the field, just minding my own business, looking for my football. That's when it happened."

"What happened?" another of his friends asked.

"I saw all of these eyes looking at me!" he cringed. "From the woods!"

"Eyes?" the girl beside him laughed. "What were they, owls?"

"No," Max said firmly. "These were no owls. When I saw them, I got scared. I started to run," he shook his head and shuddered. "But when I looked over my shoulder, those eyes were chasing me!"

"Just eyes?" the boy in front of him asked.

"No, eyes that belonged to zombies!" Max said with fear in his voice.

"Zombies can't run," the girl beside him pointed out. "I know. I've seen movies with my brother and they can't run. They just kind of stumble around."

"Well these could," Max said with a growl. "That's why when we were playing tag, I got scared."

"Wow, who knew the playground could be so spooky at night," one of his friends shivered. "I wonder why zombies would be there."

"Everybody knows that zombies like to slide," the girl beside Max nodded as if she was an expert.

"No way," some of the other kids said, but they all had fear in their eyes.

"All I'm saying," Max said sternly. "Is nobody should go to the playground at night."

The other kids all nodded, but Max could tell that some of them had decided they would.

After school the members of Mouse's secret club met up in front of the school.

"How did it go today?" Mouse asked Amanda and Max.

"Great!" Amanda said cheerfully.

"Perfect," Max nodded. "We're sure to get some kids checking it out."

"Good job," Rebekah cheered for them.

"Now we just have to get the stuff," Jaden added. "Everyone ready?"

"Absolutely!" they all cheered. Mouse was very excited about the haunted playground. He couldn't wait to put everything together and create the scariest prank ever!

FIVE

Jaden waited until his mother hung the sheets out on the line. Then he crept behind the bushes and the dog house. He watched to make sure that she had disappeared inside of the house. Then swiftly and quietly he ran up to the sheets. He grabbed as many as he could from the line. When his mother glanced out the window in the direction of the laundry, she gasped.

"Ghost!" she cried out at first as Jaden ran off across the yard. Then she realized it was her sheets running off. "Laundry thief!" she shrieked and ran out into the backyard. But Jaden was already running down the sidewalk, out of sight.

Meanwhile, Max had sneaked into his father's laboratory. His father was a scientist and liked to tinker with things at home as well. Max knew enough about the chemicals in his lab to know what was safe and what was dangerous. He also knew what glowed. As his father was typing his latest findings into his computer, Max slipped inside. He snatched a bottle that contained a mixture of chemicals that he and his father had made to fill glow sticks with. It would be perfect for the haunted playground!

On the other side of town Amanda was practicing piano. Her

grandmother was sitting on the couch enjoying the music. As Amanda expected it soon lulled her into a nap. Amanda took this time to hurry down to the basement. Here she found some old chains and metal scraps from when her brother was in a resource art phase. He would only make his sculptures out of things he found. She was careful with the metal scraps, but her brother had sanded all the sharp edges. She tried to be quiet as she carried them back up the stairs, but the chains rattled along the way. Luckily, her grandmother stayed sound asleep.

Rebekah was knee deep in her mother's garden. She was collecting something rather squirmy. In a small container she had already tossed several worms, a few beetles and an assortment of caterpillars.

"Come here you," she hissed as a long worm tried to escape into the ground.

Mouse was carefully pasting glowing yellow and red eyes on a clear shower curtain he had found. He added some fangs as well as some scary monster teeth. He made a whole row of them before he headed off to meet his friends at the tree house.

SIX

When they all gathered together in the tree house they each had their various items to show.

"Those sheets are perfect," Mouse said when Jaden held up the bundle. "But we better make sure we set some club money aside to buy your Mom some new ones."

"Yeah," Jaden's eyes widened. "I'm pretty sure she knows that I'm the laundry thief."

"I've got this," Amanda said as she held up a small chain. "And plenty more at the bottom of the tree."

"Check this out," Max said as he held up a bottle of clear liquid.

"What's so great about that?" Amanda asked with a frown.

"Watch," Max smirked as he covered the bottle with his hands. One by one the kids took a turn peering through his cupped hands at the eerie green glow the liquid produced.

"Amazing," Jaden laughed and Rebekah agreed.

"I've never seen anything like it, and I'm sure the kids that come to the haunted playground won't have either," she grinned as she looked around at her friends. "But wait until you see what I have."

She was holding a plastic purple container with the lid sealed tight. Mouse, Jaden, Amanda, and Max all leaned forward trying to see what was inside. When Rebekah lifted the lid the tree house was filled with shrieks, mostly emanating from Max, with several coming from Amanda as well.

"Rebekah!" Mouse shouted as one of the beetles made it out of the container and scuttled across the floor of the tree house. "Fake bugs! Fake bugs!" he groaned and smacked his forehead. "Not real ones!"

"Oh," Rebekah's eyes widened innocently. "Well, I'm sorry I misunderstood," she put the lid quickly back on the container and tried not to giggle at Max who was huddled in a corner as far from the container as possible. Amanda was staring in horror at the container.

"Can I look at them again?" Jaden asked as he moved to sit next to Rebekah.

"No!" Max and Amanda both shouted at the same time.

Mouse sighed. "Maybe you two could look at them outside of the club house?" he suggested.

"Sure," Rebekah grinned.

"Okay, so we'll all meet back here after dinner tonight," Mouse said sternly. "No excuses. We have to get the haunted playground set up way before Halloween so people will be less suspicious."

"I'll be here," Rebekah announced happily.

"Uh," Amanda looked at the container Rebekah was still holding.

"With fake bugs," Rebekah promised, though she still looked a little disappointed.

SEVEN

As Mouse was getting ready to meet his friends at the park, he glanced over his collection of pet mice. One in particular, a tiny white mouse with a very pink nose seemed eager to get out of his cage.

"Alright Casper," he smiled as he reached into the cage and scooped the mouse up. "You can come along for the fun."

He tucked the Mouse into his pocket along with a few bits of cheese. Once he had all the supplies they would need, he headed out to the park. Not long after he arrived, all of the other members of his secret club began arriving too. Jaden was still munching on a slice of pizza as he walked up.

"Sorry, my big sister had a pizza party," he said as he scarfed down the slice of pizza.

Casper poked his head up out of Mouse's pocket at the smell of the pizza. Max came running up with Amanda not far behind him.

"Listen I heard a bunch of kids are going to check out the haunted playground tonight," he said happily. "We need to get this set up quick!"

Rebekah was the last to arrive, tugging behind her a large bag.

"What's in there?" Amanda asked nervously as she looked at the bag.

"Bugs," Rebekah replied, her eyes shining. "Very big bugs."

"Oh great, because those creepy things need to get bigger," Max said and rolled his eyes.

"Let's see," Mouse said with a grin.

Rebekah opened the bag and everyone peaked inside. They were not just bugs, but huge bugs. They looked very real, and very hairy.

"Good job," Mouse said. He was very impressed. "Alright let's get the ghosts hung, the fishing wire strung, and the bugs in place."

"I brought something else," Amanda added as she pulled out a large hairy teddy bear.

"What's that for?" Jaden teased. "Something to hug in case you get scared?"

"No," Amanda said and stuck out her tongue at Jaden. "Look at this," she grinned and laid the teddy bear face down in the grass. With its cutesy features hidden, it just looked like a large hairy creature.

"Oh wow!" Mouse nodded his head quickly. "That's pretty scary looking."

EIGHT

The friends began working together to transform the playground from a place to play into a place to scream. As it grew darker, the glowing paint they had made from the liquid that Max supplied really began to show its magic. They painted Jaden's bedsheets with it to give their ghosts an eerie glow. They also added some to the clear shower curtain with the scary eyes and faces on it. When it hung in the air it was see through, so all they could see was the eerie glowing faces of monsters.

They strung the ghosts up in the branches of the trees with a pulley so that they could be swung up and down with a tug of a string. They also attached a few spiders to fishing wire so that they could be pulled across the sidewalk without anyone seeing the wire. When they were done the playground looked exactly the same, because all of their spooky tricks were hidden from view.

"Ready guys?" Mouse rubbed his hands together with a gleam in his eyes.

"Let's do it!" Max said and pumped his fist in the air.

The kids gathered behind the large trees just outside the playground. They heard footsteps approaching. They saw flashlight beams swinging in all directions.

"Are you sure we should go in there?" one of the boys whispered to another.

"Sure I'm sure," the other boy said boldly. "There's nothing haunted about this playground, and we're going to prove it."

With that the small group of four kids began walking into the playground. Mouse and his friends scattered in all different directions to reach their posts. It began with the howling. It came from all different directions, making the four boys look around in fear.

"What's that?" one asked.

"Wolves," another shrugged.

"Or ghosts," said the third.

"Or a tape recorder, or people hiding out," the boy in charge said with a laugh. "Don't be fooled, it's all a joke," he insisted as he walked forward. When he reached the small gathering of trees beside the playground, a glowing white spirit ghost swung down from the branches, followed by the rattling of chains and metal.

"Ah!" the boy in charge shrieked and jumped backwards. As the other boys began to cry out as well, the swings began to move back and forth on their own. Loud ear-splitting shrieks went along with their swinging.

"Ah!" all the boys were screaming now. They started running for the trees. As they ran past the slide, huge spiders went scuttling down its shiny silver surface.

"Spiders!" the shortest boy squealed and began to run faster. When they reached the trees, hoping to hide from whatever was after them, they were greeted by glowing eyes and vicious faces.

"Get out!" a booming voice said from behind the trees. "The playground is for monsters at night!"

The boys didn't have to be told twice as they went running back toward the entrance of the playground. As they ran they ran right into the thin webbing that hung across the sidewalk, stretched from one branch to another.

"Ugh, get it off!" they began shrieking and pawing at their faces. They dropped their flashlights and ran as fast they could. They were nearly at the entrance when another glowing ghost swung down to frighten them. Beside them in the grass a beastly figure began to wriggle as if it was going to jump up at them. By the time the kids made it out of the playground, they were promising to never return in the dark.

NINE

Mouse and his friends poked their heads out from where they had been hiding. They gave each other thumbs up, and then ducked back down as another crowd of kids approached. This one was much larger, with girls and boys. They had more than just flashlights too. They came armed with glow sticks, noisemakers, and even a net.

"We're going to catch ourselves a monster," the girl in charge declared. Mouse and his friends got ready to scare them. They hid behind trees, ducked behind bushes, and Rebekah disappeared beneath the slide. The group didn't get very far into the playground before the first enormous spider was pulled across the sidewalk. It caused just about all of them to jump, but there weren't too many screams. As the kids continued to move through the playground some of them began to swirl their noisemakers.

"We aren't scared of you ghosts!" the girl in the lead called out. Her friends began repeating the same words. Just then a glowing white ghost dove down from the branches above their heads.

"Ah!" some of the kids screamed and ran, but the girl in charge and two of her friends stood perfectly still. Jaden was reeling the ghost back in, when one boldly reached up and grasped the tablecloth.

"This isn't a ghost!" he said snidely and tugged at the sheet. Jaden hid behind the tree, hoping not to be spotted.

"I knew it!" the girl in charge announced. "This is just some prank someone is playing."

Mouse grimaced where he was hiding near the swings. He had hoped they wouldn't be found out so easily. From all directions howling and rattling started.

"Who's there?" the girl asked and shined her flashlight all around the playground. "Who did this?" she demanded and began looking around for hiding places. Mouse was just about to step out and admit that it was a prank, when he felt something very strange. It felt like tiny claws tickling across his feet. He gulped and started to look down. What he saw was a gigantic spider. Not just a big spider, or a large spider, or even a huge spider, but a gigantic spider!

"Ah, ah," Mouse began to shriek as he tried to shake the spider off of his show. The spider clung on to his shoe and Mouse could feel its claws getting tangled in his shoelaces. "Get off!" he finally screamed and stumbled out of his hiding place. As he did, he got caught in the shower curtain with the scary eyes and faces. It wrapped around his head as he spun around trying to free himself from the curtain as well as the spider stuck to his shoe.

"Help me!" he cried out, but with the shower curtain across his mouth it sounded strange and muffled. He stumbled out on to the sidewalk, his arms stretched out in front of him as he tried to keep his balance while trying to kick the spider off of his shoe.

"Oh no!" the girl in charge shouted when she saw him lumbering toward her. Mouse's face was covered with fangs, monster teeth, and glowing eyes. He looked like the scariest thing in the world. "Run!" she shrieked and all of the kids that were with her seemed to agree. They all bolted for the entrance of the playground.

TEN

Rebekah hurried out from underneath the slide once the coast was clear. Jaden stepped out from behind the tree. Amanda and Max came running from where they had been hiding.

"Are you okay?" Rebekah asked Mouse as she tugged the material off of his face. "What a great prank!"

"I'm not pranking!" Mouse shrieked still wiggling his foot. "Look at that spider!"

"Oh no, oh no!" Amanda looked like she might pass out, and Max ran and hid behind her. It was Jaden that was brave enough to crouch down and take a closer look at the spider.

"Mouse relax, it's just one of Rebekah's fake spiders," Jaden said with a smile and a shake of his head. "I didn't think anything could scare you."

"No it's not," Mouse insisted. "It's real!"

"Of course it's not real," Jaden argued and reached out to grab the spider. When he did the spider began to wriggle and squirm. "Ah!" Jaden sat back, his eyes wide with horror. "It is real!"

As they all watched with amazement, the spider began to crawl off of Mouse's shoe. Then out from under the spider crept Mouse's pet mouse, Casper. Jaden reached down and scooped Casper up before he could escape.

"Wow!" Mouse laughed out loud as he took his squirming pet back from Jaden. "I can't believe it. We set up this prank to scare everyone else and I have to tell you, that was the most scared I've ever been!"

"Me too," Rebekah giggled. Amanda was still trying to recover from the sight of the big spider moving. Max slowly inched out from behind her.

"So it's not real, right?" he asked as he eyed the fake spider on the ground.

"Nope it's not real," Mouse laughed again. "But I think that we can call this prank a success!"

The whole town couldn't stop talking about how scary the haunted playground was, and what an amazing prank it was. Mouse and the members of his secret club were the only ones who knew just how scary it really was!

BOOK 3: SPOTTED!

ONE

Mouse stared out the window at the sky. It was very blue. Not a cloud in sight. Not the slightest hint of snow. He sighed and laid his head down on his desk.

Mouse liked school...most of the time. He liked seeing his friends, like his best friend Rebekah and the other members of his secret club. He liked learning new things, and even taking tests. But sometimes, he just got bored.

Sometimes, he just wanted out of his desk so badly that he would do anything. Once he even volunteered to empty all the garbage cans in the school just so he could roam the halls. Another time he had asked if he could inspect the hallways while they were empty for any safety hazards or areas that needed to be fixed up.

But Mouse was running out of excuses and it didn't look like there were going to be any snow days any time soon. He had already finished his work for the class he was in and his toes would not stop wiggling in his shoes.

He thought about all of the things he could be teaching his pet mice at home. He had an assortment of mice that he trained to do various things, but they were also his friends. He always had one with him tucked away in his pocket. But when he peeked into the top pocket of his shirt his mouse was sleeping.

"You must be as bored as I am," Mouse whispered to his pet. He looked at the clock and watched the second hand tick in a slow circle. He sighed again and looked back out the window.

The green grass was calling him. The playground in the distance was likely to be empty, which meant he could play all day. The playground was also where the secret hideout of his secret club was. It was a tree house that he had stumbled upon by accident. Now it was the place where his secret club planned pranks and practical jokes. Thinking of the tree house gave him an idea. He smiled.

"Uh oh," Rebekah whispered from beside him when she saw his smile.

"What?" Mouse asked innocently.

"I know that look," Rebekah narrowed her eyes. "Just what are you planning?"

Rebekah was a great detective. Most of the time he really liked that about her. Sometimes though, it got a little annoying.

"I'm not planning anything," he insisted and tried to hide his smile.

"Lies," Rebekah hissed.

"Rebekah?" the teacher called out from the front of the class. "Did you have something that you'd like to share with the whole class?"

Rebekah sighed and shook her head. "No Mrs. Connel, I'm sorry."

"No talking in class," Mrs. Connel reminded them. "If you're bored, the blackboard could use cleaning."

Mouse jumped up out of his desk so fast that he nearly knocked it over.

"I'll do it, I'll do it," he called out eagerly.

"You can both do it," the teacher sighed and pointed them in the direction of the chalkboard. Rebekah didn't look too happy to be cleaning off the board, but Mouse was relieved to be out of his desk. As they began scrubbing off the board, Mouse whispered to her.

"Do you want to meet up after school?" he asked. "We haven't had a meeting of the secret club in a while."

"I can't today," Rebekah frowned. "My parents are having a family portrait done tomorrow after school so today my mother and I are going to get our hair styled."

"That sounds like fun," Mouse grimaced.

"It will be," Rebekah grinned.

TWO

Just then the bell rang, signaling that the school day was over. Mouse was so happy that he ran right out of the class and down the hall to his locker. When he reached his locker he spotted Jaden standing beside it.

"Hi Jaden," Mouse said happily. "Can you meet up this afternoon?"

"Sure," Jaden nodded. "I'll meet your there. I'll tell Amanda too."

"Great!" Mouse said. "I'll see if I can catch up with Max on the way out."

Mouse put his books on the shelf inside his locker and grabbed his backpack. As he hurried out the front door of the school he nearly ran right into Max who was bent over tying his shoe.

"Watch it Mouse!" Max grunted as he jumped out of the way.

"Sorry," Mouse laughed. "I was in a hurry to find you."

"Well you did," Max laughed. "What's up?"

"Can you meet up later?" Mouse asked hopefully.

"Sure," he replied with a nod. "I'll meet you over there in about a half hour."

Mouse dropped his backpack off at home and waved to his

mother as he ran right back out the door. She laughed, "Don't be late for dinner!" she called out.

Mouse ran straight for the park. He was disappointed that Rebekah wouldn't be able to be there, but he was still happy to get together with his friends. He had a wonderful idea for a prank brewing and he couldn't wait to share it.

When he arrived at the tree house, he found that he was the first one there. He climbed up to the large wooden shack and ducked inside.

There was enough room for them all to fit along with a little space for some extras, like the book of pranks he had found when he first discovered the tree house and a stash of snacks. Mouse slipped his pet into a small cage he kept in the tree house. His mice weren't used to high places so he had to keep them safe. It wasn't long before Amanda came climbing up.

"Hi Mouse," she said with a smile. "What are you planning?" she asked when she saw the smile on his lips.

"Why does everyone keep asking me that?" Mouse asked with a grin.

"Oh you're up to something," Amanda said with a shake of her head. "Do you want to tell me about it now or are we waiting for everyone else?" she asked.

"Everyone except Rebekah," Mouse nodded.

"We're here!" Jaden called out as he climbed up to the tree house, with Max climbing right behind him.

"Good, I'm glad you guys are all here," Mouse said as he took a seat and waited for his friends to do the same.

THREE

"This is an official meeting of Mouse's Secret Club," he said firmly. This statement let his friends know that anything he said after was completely confidential, not to be shared with anyone outside of the club. "I think we need a plan to get us all a few days off of school," Mouse grinned.

"Huh?" Amanda narrowed her eyes suspiciously as she looked at Mouse. "What kind of plan would get us out of school?"

"I have a math test tomorrow," Max said quickly.

"I'm up for it," Jaden grinned. "I'd love an early weekend!"

"Alright, well here's the plan," Mouse said and leaned forward to whisper to them. "So, we all know that if one of us gets sick, it spreads, right?"

"Sure," Max nodded. "Especially if you cough on each other."

"Ew," Amanda sighed.

"What's the plan?" Jaden asked eagerly.

"Well we can't actually get sick," Mouse explained. "What fun would a few days off be if we were actually sick? We just have to make it look like we're sick, and that not only are we sick, but that it's spreading," he grinned at this.

"I don't know," Jaden said hesitantly. "This sounds like the kind of plan that ends in detention."

"Don't worry," Mouse assured him. "They will be so busy trying to make sure that the whole school doesn't catch it, that they won't have time to be suspicious."

"Uh," Amanda cleared her throat. "This all sounds great, but also impossible."

"Think about it," Mouse said with a smirk.

"Are you talking about faking a cold or something?" Max asked with confusion.

"No, colds will just get us a trip to the doctor or some medicine," Mouse said with a shudder. "What we need is something so shocking that nobody wants to come anywhere near us."

"And how exactly are you going to come up with something like that?" Max asked.

"Well Max, that's where you come in," Mouse grinned.

"Uh oh," Max frowned. Max's father was a scientist and Max's basement was his own personal lab. There were many concoctions, and Max had learned quite a bit from watching his father work. "What are you thinking?" Max asked, a little afraid, and a little curious.

"Listen," Mouse said and lowered his voice. "For this to work, no one can know. Not even Rebekah. Understand?"

All three of his friends nodded. As Mouse began to detail the plan, each one seemed a little shocked. But in the end, they agreed to all take part in his scheme. By the time they left the tree house, they were all whispering and laughing about what would happen.

FOUR

As Mouse walked back toward his house, he noticed Rebekah standing out front.

"What do you think?" she asked as she twirled so he could see her neatly curled red hair.

"It looks, uh, bouncy," Mouse said and scratched his head a little.

"I guess that's a good thing," Rebekah laughed. "Where have you been?"

"Oh I just had a quick meeting with the club," Mouse explained hesitantly.

"You didn't plan anything without me, did you?" Rebekah frowned.

"You'll see," Mouse grinned.

"No fair!" Rebekah protested and crossed her arms.

"Trust me," Mouse insisted. "This is one plan you'll be glad you were left out of."

"Okay," Rebekah replied reluctantly. She did trust Mouse, but she hated to be left out of anything. As Mouse waved goodbye to her, he hoped he hadn't hurt her feelings. But he knew that she would understand when the plan unfolded. As he closed the door to his room he grinned. He was sure that he would be getting a few extra days to enjoy schedule-free fun.

FIVE

The next day Mouse walked into school with a spring in his step. He happily collected his books and headed off to his first class, which was science. He really enjoyed his teacher, Mr. Lanister, but that wasn't why he was so happy. He was happy because he was about to pull the best prank ever.

As he walked into class Mr. Lanister greeted him with a nod and then looked back down at his lesson plan. In Science class two students shared one large desk. Mouse shared his desk with Rebekah, which was a very good thing. He needed to keep a close eye on her to make sure everything went smoothly.

"Today class, we're going to discuss what it means to be contagious," the teacher said as he walked to the front of the class. "I'm sure you've all been told by your parents or teachers to cover your mouth when you cough," he said, and then coughed into a closed fist. "This is actually not the best way to cover your mouth, because you are coughing your germs into your hand-"

As he continued to lecture the class about the proper way to prevent germs from spreading, Mouse pulled a cloth and a small bottle of liquid out of his backpack.

"What's that?" Rebekah asked curiously as she looked at the bottle.

"Shh," Mouse winked lightly at her. He waited until Mr. Lanister had finished his speech and then raised his hand.

"Yes?" Mr. Lanister asked and pointed at Mouse.

"Mr. Lanister, I brought something with me today and I'd like to try it out if that's okay with you," Mouse said quickly.

"What is it?" Mr. Lanister asked suspiciously.

"Well, it's a special solution that's designed to reveal just how many germs are on our skin," he explained as he walked toward the front of the class. "It's odorless and harmless," he added and let Mr. Lanister sniff the liquid in the bottle.

"Mouse, that sounds clever, but it's not possible," Mr. Lanister warned.

SIX

"Can I demonstrate?" Mouse asked hopefully.

"Well," Mr. Lanister hesitated. "I suppose, but only on those students that volunteer," he said firmly. "Are you sure this stuff is safe?"

Mouse leaned closer to Mr. Lanister and whispered beside his ear. "It's just a little soap and water. I don't think some extra face washing will hurt anyone."

Mr. Lanister grinned at that and nodded. "Alright Mouse, give it a shot," he said and winked heavily at Mouse.

"Any volunteers?" Mouse asked as he looked over the classroom. Rebekah immediately shot her hand up into the air.

"Okay then," Mouse cleared his throat. "Anyone other than Rebekah?"

Rebekah glared at him with frustration. He could tell that now she was really feeling left out.

"I'll try it," Sam said from the next table over.

"Okay Sam, step right up," Mouse instructed. When Sam stopped in front of him, Mouse dabbed some of the solution on to the rag. Then he wiped it on Sam's face, and hands.

"That stuff is cold," Sam complained. "Is anything happening?"

"Looks like you're germ free," Mouse grinned. Once the other students saw that Sam had not suffered any terrible consequences for raising his hand, they began to volunteer too.

"Me next, me next," Gretta said from the table in the back. One by one, Mouse wiped the faces and hands of all the students in the class, except for Rebekah.

"Wow, amazing," Mouse shook his head as he looked at the students in his class. "All of you are germ free!"

"I bet that stuff just doesn't work," Sam said with a scowl.

"I think what Mouse was trying to prove," Mr. Lanister explained as he stepped forward. "Is that washing your hands and face on a regular basis is the best way to stay germ free."

"Oh Mouse!" Gretta moaned and shook her head. "It's always a trick with you!"

Mouse smirked and took a slight bow, then under his breath he whispered. "You have no idea." As Mouse walked back to his seat, Rebekah refused to look at him.

"Don't be mad," Mouse pleaded quietly.

"I'm not mad," she said as she scribbled on a piece of paper. "I'll figure out what you're up to."

Mouse grinned and sat back to listen to the rest of the lesson on germs.

SEVEN

When Mouse walked into his gym class he found the whole place in chaos. About half the kids in the gym were pulled aside and Mr. Sparrow the gym teacher seemed to be panicking.

Mouse smirked and waved to Amanda who was in the group of kids. She turned her head toward him, revealing the dark green spots all over her face. She winked at him, and then looked back at the panicking teacher.

"Go to the nurse," he said swiftly. "No wait, you should be quarantined. How did this happen?" he gasped out. As Mouse walked closer he could see that the spots were all over the faces of the kids standing in front of the gym teacher.

"Oh no! Not you too!" Mr. Sparrow cried out as he looked at Mouse.

"What do you mean?" Mouse asked with surprise. Amanda whipped a compact out of her purse and opened it up so that Mouse could see his reflection. All over his face were the same dark green spots.

"Ah! What is happening?" Mouse gasped and wiped at his face.

Before Mr. Sparrow could answer the nurse came rushing into

the gym. "What's going on here?" she asked as she hurried over to Mr. Sparrow.

"Just take a look," Mr. Sparrow said, shaking his head with disbelief. As the nurse looked at all of the children, she soon discovered that each one was covered with these dark green spots.

"It must be marker," she murmured and pulled handi-wipe out of her pocket. She pulled Mouse close to her and reached up to scrub at the dots on his cheek. Mouse stood perfectly still, but when the spots wouldn't even smudge, the nurse began rubbing harder.

"Ouch," Mouse complained and ducked his head.

"They're not coming off," the nurse said in a high-pitched voice. "I wonder if any other students are experiencing this."

She didn't have to wonder for long. The principal's voice came over the PA system.

"Nurse Barbara, Nurse Barbara, please report to the principal's office," he said in an urgent tone.

"Oooh," some of the kids gasped and hid their smiles as if the nurse was getting in trouble. But Mouse knew what was really happening. He smirked as the kids compared the dots on their hands and faces.

"I have to go," Nurse Barbara said with a frown.

"What am I supposed to do with them?" Mr. Sparrow asked with wide eyes.

"Uh, just keep them away from the other students," Nurse Barbara said with a shake of her head.

"What about me?" Mr. Sparrow asked as he inspected the palms of his hands for any dots that might have popped up.

"Don't worry, we'll get this all figured out," Nurse Barbara assured him and hurried out of the gym.

EIGHT

"Okay, anybody with green polka dots sit on the bleachers," Mr. Sparrow said quickly. "And don't touch me!" he added.

The kids with the green spots assembled on the bleachers while the kids without them could only stare at the scene. Amanda sat down beside Mouse and shot him a grin. "I think it worked," she whispered.

"Shh," Mouse said and shook his head. She wasn't the best at keeping secrets, but Mouse could see that she was trying.

"Do you think we'll get to go home early?" a kid not far from them asked. Mouse smiled at that.

"I don't think they're going to let us go anywhere," a younger boy gasped out. His eyes were wide with fear. "They're going to lock us up. They won't let us near other kids, they won't let us see our families-"

"That's not going to happen," Mouse said firmly. "It's just a little rash or something," he tried to assure the boy.

"No, no! I've seen a movie like this!" the boy said and shuddered. "We must have some new disease from mosquitoes, or maybe from the cafeteria food!"

"It's not a new disease," Amanda said quickly, and then covered her mouth.

"Look," Mouse sighed as he spoke to the other kids who were starting to get really nervous about the green spots on their faces. "All that's going to happen is we'll get a few days off from school. No one's throwing up, no one has a fever," he pointed out.

"How do you know?" a girl in the top row of the bleachers asked. "My tummy feels funny," she groaned and stood up. All the kids seated below her began to shriek and scatter to avoid the possible vomit.

"Uh Mouse," Amanda looked over at him with a grimace. "Maybe this wasn't such a good idea."

"It'll be fine," he promised her, but even he got up and moved out of the way, just in case.

"This is crazy!" Mr. Sparrow said as he tried to herd the kids back on to the bleachers. "That's it! You kids need to go home! I'm going to speak to the principal. Nobody move," he warned them all.

"But Mr. Sparrow," the girl at the top of the bleachers groaned.

"Unless you need to throw up," Mr. Sparrow sighed. "Then of course, you can move."

"Oh good," she sighed and rubbed her belly.

"I don't know Mouse," Amanda said in a whisper. "I think this is really starting to get out of hand. Maybe we should tell them the truth?" she suggested and looked at her friend fearfully.

"It's fine," he promised her. "I'll go keep an eye on the principal," he stood up from the bleachers. "You keep an eye on them."

"I will," Amanda frowned.

NINE

All of the kids seemed to be getting a little upset about the green spots on their faces. Mouse felt a little guilty as he sneaked down the hall toward the principal's office. But he knew they weren't really sick, and neither was he.

When he reached the principal's office, he listened in to the conversation he was having with nurse Barbara and Mr. Sparrow.

"This isn't good," the principal said. "Whatever this illness is, it's spreading like wildfire through the school. Students in almost every class are showing signs of it. If we keep the kids at school they might continue to spread it and then we'll have a real problem on our hands."

"So let's send them home," Mr. Sparrow insisted. "We don't want the staff catching it too, do we?" he asked with a frown.

"No, we don't," the principal agreed. "Then we'll have to start contacting parents to pick the children up. I just wish I had some idea as to what the spots were so that I could tell them. I've never seen anything like this."

"Neither have I," nurse Barbara admitted. "I've been a school nurse for a very long time. I've seen all kinds of spots and rashes and these don't look like anything I've ever seen before."

"I just hope it's nothing serious," the principal frowned. "And to think we were just starting out our month of germ awareness."

"This isn't caused by a germ," another voice in the room said. Mouse cringed as he realized that it was Mr. Lanister, his science teacher. He hadn't expected Mr. Lanister to be involved.

"Then what?" the nurse asked. "An allergy?"

"I don't think so," Mr. Lanister shook his head. "At least, not exactly. It would be best to send the students home. They don't have any signs of illness. No fever, no fatigue. I doubt they are contagious. So these spots must be spreading by other means."

"Other means?" Mr. Sparrow asked with disbelief. "How else could they be spreading."

"I think that's something I need to speak to one particular student about," Mr. Lanister said with a sigh. Mouse's eyes widened as he heard that.

TEN

He quickly headed back toward the gym. He hoped that parents would be called before he was asked into the office. As he was halfway back to the gym, he spotted Rebekah walking toward the office. She looked a little upset.

"Rebekah what's wrong?" Mouse asked with a frown.

"I just got called to the principal's office," she said with a sniffle. "I think I'm in trouble for something."

"What? Why would you be in trouble?" Mouse asked with concern.

"I don't know. Maybe because I'm the only one out of our whole science class that doesn't have those," she pointed at Mouse's face. "What did you do Mouse?" she asked with a glare.

"It's going to be fine," Mouse promised her.

"If I get another detention, I'm going to be in serious trouble," Rebekah said.

"You won't," he promised her.

"I hope not," she sighed and continued down the hall. Mouse was really beginning to feel pretty terrible about what was supposed to be a fun prank. Between kids getting scared over the spots and Rebekah possibly getting into trouble, Mouse wondered if it would be a worth a few days off.

When he got back to the gym, more kids had been herded in from other classrooms. They all had the green spots, including Jaden and Max.

"Hey Mouse," Jaden said with a grin. "I see you've been spotted."

"Haha," Max laughed. "It worked!" he added in a whisper. "Everyone's getting sent home."

"Great," Mouse said with a sigh.

"Why aren't you happy?" Jaden asked. "Wasn't this the plan?"

"Sure it was," Mouse nodded. "I guess I just didn't expect everyone to take it so seriously."

"Well, the important thing is it worked," Max said with a nod. "No one is really sick and no one is going to get into any real trouble. So we'll get a few days off to have some fun."

Mouse nodded, but he still felt bad. He thought about telling Mr. Sparrow the truth when he walked back into the gym, but he looked so mad that Mouse decided not to.

ELEVEN

Once all of the parents had been contacted the kids began lining up outside to wait for their parents to pick them up. Mouse was standing at the edge of the circular drive watching for his mother's car. Rebekah walked up to him.

"Your mom is picking me up to," she said gruffly and crossed her arms.

"Oh good," Mouse said with a smile, but Rebekah did not smile back. "You're not still mad are you?" he asked. "What happened with the principal?"

"He asked me why I was the only one who didn't have green spots. I told him I didn't know," she sighed. "But I'm not sure that he believed me."

"Did you get into trouble?" Mouse asked with concern.

"No," she shook her head. "They're sending everyone home as a precaution."

"So why are you mad?" he asked and tried to cheer her up. "We get a half day and I bet we don't have to go to school tomorrow!"

"I'm mad because whatever you did, you left me out," she huffed and glared at him.

"Rebekah," Mouse shook his head. "I didn't leave you out to be mean. I just didn't think green spots would look good in your family portrait."

Rebekah gasped as she suddenly remembered the portrait her family had planned to take that afternoon. If she had shown up with green spots it would have been ruined.

"Oh," she said as she realized that Mouse had a good reason for leaving her out.

"Well whatever you've done, it's pretty clever," Rebekah finally smiled.

"Thanks," Mouse said proudly. "Max helped a lot on this one."

When Mouse's mother pulled up to the school she gasped at the sight of the spots on his face.

"What happened?" she asked as he and Rebekah climbed into the back seat.

"It's okay Mom," Mouse said quickly. "Nothing serious."

"I think green spots are pretty serious," she said with a huff. 'You're going straight to the doctor."

Mouse sighed as his plan certainly was not working very well.

"It's okay, really," Rebekah said. "Nobody has a fever or anything, no coughing, no sneezing. And I'm sure that the doctor will be busy with all of the other spotted kids," she added.

"Well," Mouse's mother frowned. "Alright, but you are to rest young man. Nothing but video games and movies for you!"

Mouse winked lightly at Rebekah who had to hide a smile.

The rest of the afternoon was a real treat for Mouse as he and Rebekah watched movies until her mother picked her up.

"Mouse I hope you feel better soon," Rebekah's mother said when she saw the spots on his face.

"I'm sure I will," Mouse smiled back.

After Rebekah left, Mouse found his mother in the kitchen. She had her computer open and was browsing medical sites.

"No one has ever had green spots," she said suspiciously. Then she looked up at Mouse. "Did you have something to do with this Mouse?"

Mouse widened his eyes innocently.

"How could I infect the whole school with green spots Mom?" he asked in return.

"Hm,' his mother narrowed her eyes and looked back at the computer.

When Mouse went to bed that night he felt badly again. He wondered if all of the parents were as worried as his mother. Maybe this prank really had been going a little too far.

TWELVE

When Mouse woke up the next morning he was surprised that his alarm hadn't gone off. His mice were squeaking loudly for their morning treat of cheese. Mouse tossed a few crumbs into their cage and then headed down to the kitchen.

"Morning Mouse," she said with a smile. "No school for you today."

Mouse sighed. It was exactly what he had hoped to hear and yet it didn't make him happy. He wondered how many kids were being taken to the doctor, and how many were worried that they might get worse. He knew what he had to do.

"Mom, I think I better go to school today," he said with a frown.

"Why?" his mother asked with surprise.

"I just do," he sighed. Then he walked over to his backpack.

He pulled out a small bottle of solution, a different solution than what he had used before. He poured some of the liquid on a napkin and wiped it across his cheek. When he pulled the napkin away, the green spots were wiped away. He held out the napkin to show her the green smudges that were left behind.

"Mouse," she sighed. "I'll drive you to school."

Mouse got dressed quickly and tucked one of his mice into his front top pocket for moral support. When he arrived at school, he was surprised to find Rebekah, Jaden, Amanda and Max waiting for him.

"What are you guys doing here?" he asked.

"I knew you would end up telling the truth," Rebekah explained.

"And we were all part of this," Jaden said firmly. "You shouldn't have to do it alone."

"Thanks," Mouse said with relief. It was nice to know that he had such good friends. As they walked toward the principal's office with their heads hanging down, the door to the science classroom swung open. Mr. Lanister reached out and pulled Mouse inside. His friends followed after him.

"That was some trick Mouse," Mr. Lanister said. He had green spots all over his face. "I figured it out," he grinned.

"You did?" Mouse asked with surprise as he looked at the green spots on his teacher's face.

"Yes, first I suspected Rebekah because she was the only one in the class without spots. But then I remembered that you were the one who washed everyone's face and hands in class. Then I heard from other teachers, that your friends here had done the same stunt in their classes. So I found the rags and I tested them.

How clever Max," he said as he looked right at Max, and then back at Mouse. "That you figured out a combination that would only activate with body heat. So as the solution warmed, the spots began to appear. To all of us it looked like some horrible rash spreading through the school."

"I know," Mouse frowned. "I didn't really think about that part."

"We were going to the principal," Jaden added. Amanda was staring hard at the floor.

"We just thought it would be a fun way to get a few days off," Mouse explained.

"Well, it wasn't fun," Mr. Lanister said. "Not for the kids who had to go to the doctor, and not for the teachers who will be behind in their lesson plans now. But," he paused a moment and all of the kids looked up at him. "I think you've learned a pretty good lesson.

I already created the solution that would clean the green spots and gave it to the principal who is handing it out to parents as they bring their kids in.

Just this once," he looked right into Mouse's eyes. "I'm going to keep this little prank to myself. But to make up for what you've done, you're all going to spend Saturday helping to clean up the school and make sure it is germ free."

"On a Saturday?" Mouse gasped.

"On every Saturday for the rest of this month," Mr. Lanister corrected. "Unless you'd rather I tell the principal?" he suggested.

"No!" all of the kids shouted together.

Mouse and his friends had to spend an extra day a week in school, but that gave them plenty of time to plan their next prank. Only next time, it wouldn't include green spots.

BOOK 4: MAGNIFICENT MARVIN

ONE

Mouse was walking home from school one day when it happened. He stopped dead in his tracks and stared straight ahead. His eyes were stuck on something spectacular.

It had been nearly a year and Mouse had almost forgotten about it with all the pranks that he and his secret club had been playing around town and at school. But right there before him was an amazing sight. When he saw it he jumped up and down and shouted as he thrust his fist into the air.

"Yes! Yes! The carnival is coming to town!" he shouted for everyone in the neighborhood to hear. Other kids, even those a few streets over, began cheering as well. Mouse ran all the way home, his mind filling with ideas. He knew for sure that this year would be the year that his plan would finally happen.

As soon as he reached the house, he called the other members of his secret club to plan an emergency meeting. Within an hour, Mouse, Jaden, Rebekah, Amanda and Max were huddled together in the tree house that they used as their secret clubhouse, plotting out their next, and in Mouse's opinion, most important prank.

The shimmering lights that stood out against the night sky looked like stars. But they weren't. They were the first sign that the carnival had finally arrived in town. All year Mouse waited for the carnival. He liked Christmas just fine, and his birthday was always great, but there was nothing more exciting to him than the carnival coming to town.

Not only did he enjoy the rides and tasty carnival food like triple chili hot dogs and deep fried oreos, but he really loved the Magnificent Marvin act.

Magnificent Marvin had been in the carnival every year that Mouse had gone. He was a magician, but he was so much more than that. He tricked all of his audience members into believing one thing and then presented them with something much different. Mouse admired the way that he was able to be fooled by him every time, but this year was going to be different. Mouse was determined that it would be.

He had enlisted the help of his friends in his secret club. His best friend, Rebekah, along with his friends Jaden, Max, and Amanda, had all agreed to help him pull the ultimate prank on Magnificent Marvin.

TWO

As they arrived at the carnival they discovered that everyone else in town had decided to come out for the event as well. The fairgrounds were packed with people, from the very old to the very young, who were all looking forward to a very fun evening.

Mouse had a very special box tucked under his arm. It contained three of his favorite mice. Each one had its own special talent.

Magellan was a great explorer and would navigate any maze he was put into. Houdini was a great escape artist who managed to find his way out of just about any cage he was in. Finally, Takahashi was his fastest mouse. He moved so swiftly that even Mouse had a hard time catching up with him.

"Are you sure this is going to work?" Amanda asked nervously as she heard the mice scratching in the box.

"If we all do our part then it'll definitely work," Mouse said with confidence. Rebekah came running up from the other side of the carnival. She had arrived a little earlier to plan out her part of the prank.

"Are the mice ready?" she asked with excitement.

"Yes they are," Mouse nodded with a grin. "We ran through the drill three times. But where are Max and Jaden?" he wondered as he searched the crowd of carnival goers.

"We're here!" Max called out as the two boys hurried over to Rebekah and Mouse. "Sorry, I-"

"He just scarfed down a chili cheese dog!" Jaden reported with wide eyes. "I've never seen someone eat something so fast!"

"Wow!" Mouse laughed and shook his head. "I'm pretty impressed Max."

"Thanks," Max said and rubbed his stomach. "It was so very good."

"I can't wait to get some cotton candy," Amanda declared eagerly.

"Don't worry, when this prank is over, there will be plenty of time for snacks," Mouse assured them all. "And games," he added as Rebekah's eyes had wandered over to a giant stuffed parrot hanging from one of the game booths.

"Are you sure that we're ready for this?" Jaden asked hopefully. "I mean it sounds good on paper, but do you really think it will work?"

"Everything's in place," Rebekah said confidently.

"It's going to be perfect," Mouse assured them all. "The first part of the mission is the only one that really matters, because if we don't accomplish that, then we're not going to be able to pull any of this off."

"Oh don't worry," Amanda grinned as she whipped out a few small containers. "I am ready to make sure that mission is accomplished. Hands please!" she called out. All of the kids held out their hands.

THREE

A few booths away Mouse spotted Magnificent Marvin. He was already performing his first show and taunting the audience.

"No one plays better tricks than Magnificent Marvin," he informed his audience. "Prepare to be marveled!"

The audience cheered and Mouse smirked. Every year he had heard that same speech from Magnificent Marvin, but this year he was determined to make sure that Magnificent Marvin experienced the flip side of his promise.

"You're going down Magnificent Marvin," Mouse muttered under his breath.

"All set!" Amanda declared to the others and they began walking toward Magnificent Marvin's booth to take their places in the audience before the next show could get started.

They gathered close as Magnificent Marvin whipped his cape dramatically around him. He spoke in a low haunting voice that made Mouse's eyes widen. He had been trying to get his voice to get that low, but so far it only managed to squeak, much like the mice he kept as pets.

"Are you ready to be dazzled? Are you ready to be amazed?"

Magnificent Marvin asked with a sparkle in his eyes as he peered at his audience over the edge of his cape.

"Yes!" the crowd cheered and clapped. Most of them had seen Magnificent Marvin's act before but they were eager to see it again.

"Good, because you will be!" Magnificent Marvin declared with complete certainty.

"May I please have a volunteer?" Magnificent Marvin inquired with a shimmer in his gaze. "But be warned," he held up a hand to stop the eagerness of the crowd. "If you volunteer, prepare to be humiliated, prepare to be embarrassed, prepare to be left in awe of the absolute magnificence that is Marvin!"

Mouse smirked as he narrowed his eyes. He was willing to accept the challenge. "Now, volunteers?" Magnificent Marvin asked and swept his gaze over the audience.

Everyone in the crowd had their hands up, but Mouse and Amanda had made a plan to get noticed. Rebekah, Amanda, Max, Jaden, as well as mouse had all coated their hands with glitter, so that the flashing lights of the carnival would dance off of their hands. The plan was that no matter who was picked, that person would defer to Mouse, and ask that he take their place.

Jaden was jumping up and down waving his hand in the air. Max was standing right up front waving his hand like a windshield wiper back and forth in front of Magnificent Marvin. Rebekah was standing amidst the smaller kids so that she would be noticed before they were. Amanda was bouncing up and down and shouting, "Over here, me, me, me," she wouldn't normally behave this way of course, but this was for Mouse.

Mouse was standing at the back of the crowd, his hand casually raised, waiting for one of the others to be chosen. However, Magnificent Marvin looked directly at him, as if he had been looking for him in particular.

FOUR

"You there," Magnificent Marvin said as he pointed to Mouse. "All the way in the back," he said quickly. "Yes you. You look like a young man that can take a joke," he grinned at Mouse. Mouse arched an eyebrow with a friendly smile. He hoped that Magnificent Marvin could take a joke as well.

As he walked up to the stage the rest of the crowd moaned in disappointment. Mouse spotted several of his other friends from school and they were cheering for him. Everyone knew that Mouse had a habit of getting in trouble for the pranks that he liked to pull.

Of course no one knew that he had started a whole secret club for the purpose of pulling pranks. He knew that the other members of Mouse's Secret Club were now taking their positions to make this the greatest prank ever. At least until they thought of the next one.

As Magnificent Marvin looked Mouse directly in the eyes, Mouse couldn't help but smirk a little.

"Now, what's your name young man?" he asked with a wide smile.

"It's Mouse," Mouse replied with a slight shrug. He felt Houdini wiggling around inside of the front pocket of his shirt.

"Mouse?" Magnificent Marvin repeated with wide eyes. "That's not true. Don't try to fool Magnificent Marvin! Tell me the truth. What's your name boy?"

Mouse's smirk spread into a wide smile. "It's Mouse," he repeated. Magnificent Marvin narrowed his eyes and leaned closer to Mouse.

"Ah, we've got a jokester do we?" he grinned at that. "A kindred spirit, I'd guess?" he asked with a light wink.

"Uh sure, whatever that is," Mouse replied as casually as he could. He was trying not to burst out into laughter as he knew what was about to unfold.

"Alright then, Mouse, meet my mouse, Mikey," Magnificent Marvin revealed a small silver box that had a small maze designed inside of it. In the middle of the maze was a small white mouse which didn't look much different than Mouse's pet Houdini.

"He is the smartest mouse in the world," Magnificent Marvin announced. Then he blinked and added, "No offense Mouse, I'm sure you're smart too."

The audience roared with laughter and Mouse blushed a little. "Why's he so smart?" Mouse asked, knowing that it was part of the ruse as he had seen the act so many times before.

FIVE

"Well he can do tricks," Marvin explained and set the box down. He reached into the box and pulled out his mouse. He set the mouse down on the table in front of him. With a swish of his hand he hid the fact that he had placed a piece of cheese against his palm.

"Alright Mikey, walk!" Marvin commanded and waved his hand with a flourish over the mouse. Mikey rose up on his hind feet and began walking toward the scent of the cheese. To the audience, he was just walking towards Marvin's hand.

"Now dance Mikey, dance!" Marvin demanded and then waved his hand in a slow circle above the mouse. Mikey spun in the same slow circle, his little eyes fixed on the piece of cheese. The audience clapped with amazement.

"That's not all!" Marvin announced and led Mikey over to a small obstacle course he had set up. Mikey jumped over, crawled under, and even laid flat on his back, all by Marvin's command, or at least his desire for the cheese in his hand.

Again the audience clapped and cheered for the amazing mouse, who seemed to be under Marvin's spell. Mouse waited patiently until Magnificent Marvin turned to look at him once more.

"So what do you think Mouse? Who's smarter?" he asked with a gleam in his eye.

"Well," Mouse replied thoughtfully. "I have a trick I can do too," he smiled.

"Oh please son, don't embarrass yourself," Marvin said with a chuckle. "It's Magnificent Marvin, not Magnificent Mouse!"

"It'll only take a second," Mouse pleaded as he looked up at the man. "I mean, I don't think the audience would mind seeing one more trick. Do you?" he batted his eyes innocently.

The audience began to cheer for the strange boy on the stage, thanks to the few classmates of Mouse's that were still scattered through the crowd. Marvin looked a little impatient, but Mouse knew he would give in. The first rule of entertainment was to give the audience what they wanted, no matter what.

SIX

"Fine," Magnificent Marvin finally relented. "One quick trick, okay? But don't be disappointed if you can't fool me," he added with a scowl. "No one ever has."

"Sure, sure," Mouse nodded a little. Then he reached into his pocket. He stood very close to Magnificent Marvin as he pulled out a piece of cheese. He dusted off the lint from his pocket and held it up for the audience to see.

"I can make a piece of cheese disappear!" he announced with a proud grin. Magnificent Marvin rolled his eyes and looked away.

"Do it! Do it!" the audience chanted. Marvin waved his hand dismissively, as if it was no big deal that Mouse might make some cheese disappear. So Mouse popped the piece of cheese right into his mouth and swallowed it.

Half of the audience stared in stunned silence, while the other half began to boo and heckle Mouse. Marvin laughed in an attempt to make light of the act. But before he could laugh too hard, Houdini tugged free of Mouse's front pocket. He lunged for the cheese tucked in Marvin's palm and snatched it right into his mouth.

"Hey!" Marvin bellowed as Houdini landed in the small silver maze that had housed Mikey. "Give me back that cheese!" Marvin demanded. The audience began to laugh and heckle, though some looked genuinely confused. Every time Marvin tried to get a hold of Houdini, Houdini dodged right out of the way. Then he climbed over the edge of the box and jumped down to the stage.

"Stop that mouse!" Marvin demanded as Houdini began running to the edge of the stage.

"I'm not doing anything!" Mouse declared innocently, adding more chaos to the moment.

"Not you Mouse, your mouse!" Marvin hollered.

"I know I'm Mouse," Mouse tilted his head slightly to the side. "Are you okay Magnificent Marvin?"

"No!" Marvin shouted loudly. "Not YOU are Mouse! Your mouse! Stop your mouse!"

"I think you're confused," Mouse chuckled lightly.

SEVEN

Marvin growled and chased after Houdini, who was quickly escaping into the audience of onlookers. Mouse was starting to laugh so hard that he could barely keep up with Marvin who was charging through the audience after the mouse.

Some of the less mouse friendly members of the audience were shrieking and jumping up on their chairs. They were making quite a commotion, even though the carnival rides and music were loud. Mouse had to keep up to make sure that Houdini ran in the right direction.

Magnificent Marvin chased after Houdini in a panic.

"Come back here with my cheese!" he hollered as he ran after the mouse. Rebekah saw him coming around the corner of the mirror maze and grinned. Houdini raced straight toward the small corridor that Rebekah had built.

Magellan was waiting at the end of the corridor. When he smelled the cheese that Houdini was carrying, he battled with Houdini for it. Just as Magnificent Marvin reached down to scoop up Houdini, Magellan snatched the cheese from Houdini.

He turned with the cheese safely in his mouth and ran down the long wooden corridor.

"Blast!" Magnificent Marvin grumbled as he began to chase after Magellan. Jaden bent down and scooped up Houdini before he could escape.

"Good job little guy," he grinned. Magellan ran all the way to the end of the corridor and up a ramp, into the Maze of Mirrors.

EIGHT

"No!" Magnificent Marvin cried out. "Not in there!" he huffed and chased after the sprinting mouse. Magellan had already disappeared into the Maze of Mirrors.

"Oh so sorry," Mouse was calling out from behind Magnificent Marvin. "Let me help you find him!" he offered as he followed Magnificent Marvin into the Maze of Mirrors.

"No, no, no," Magnificent Marvin shook his head as the mirrors reflected at least a dozen mice. They also reflected a dozen Magnificent Marvins, and a dozen reflections of Mouse who had run up behind him. "I have to get that cheese back," he insisted. "It is the only cheese that my mouse will respond to and we have shows to do all evening!"

"Don't worry, we'll get it back!" Mouse said, trying not to laugh. He knew that Magnificent Marvin was certainly getting a taste of his own medicine. As they began making their way through the maze, he could only hope that Max was doing his part on the outside.

Max was waiting by the exit of the Maze of Mirrors. He had a box ready to scoop Magellan into. He also had a small plastic cage in which Takahashi waited to do his part in the mission.

When he heard Magnificent Marvin's voice from inside the Maze of Mirrors, he knew that they were getting closer to the exit. As he crouched down with the box ready to scoop, he hoped that Magellan would be able to live up to his name.

Magellan scampered right out of the Maze of Mirrors and down the small ramp to where Max was waiting. Max scooped up Magellan with the box. Then he opened up the cage and let Magellan scurry inside.

Magellan and Takahashi tussled over the piece of cheese for a moment before Takahashi finally won. Once Takahashi had the piece of cheese firmly in his mouth, Max let him free of the cage. Takahashi ran so fast down the second wooden corridor that Rebekah had built, that all Max saw was a white blur.

"Wait! Come back!" Magnificent Marvin called out as he ran out of the Maze of Mirrors. Mouse was right behind him. He winked and waved at Max as he ran past who winked and waved in return. He also gave him a thumbs up to let Mouse know that everything was going according to plan.

NINE

Poor Marvin was completely out of breath and had to pause for a moment to draw in some air.

"Oh dear, are you okay?" Mouse asked and patted the man's back gingerly. "Do you need some water perhaps?" Mouse asked kindly. Marvin nodded his head, gasping for breath.

"Jaden! Water!" Mouse cried out loudly. Jaden who had been waiting for his cue came running up with a cup of water, but he pretended to trip and sloshed the cup of water right into Marvin's face.

"Ah!" Marvin cried out and sputtered as he tried to wipe the water off of his face.

"Poor thing!" Amanda called out as she rushed over to them. "Would you like a rag to clean off your face?" she smiled as she offered him the rag.

"Oh thank you. Finally," he huffed and glowered at Jaden. "Someone with manners," he began wiping the rag across his face to clean off the water. What he didn't know was that the rag had been covered in glitter, and when he was done wiping it, so was his face.

He handed the rag back to Amanda with a grateful smile and

then began running after Takahashi once more. As fast as he tried to run, the mouse always seemed to be much faster.

By the time the mouse reached the end of the wooden corridor, the crowd of onlookers had caught wind of what was happening. Some were cheering the mouse on, while others were cheering on Magnificent Marvin.

Takahashi ran right up the small ramp to the stage. Mikey, who had been forgotten in the middle of his obstacle course, had made his way down to the stage from the table. When he saw Takahashi barreling toward him, he ducked down, a little frightened. Takahashi still had the piece of cheese in his mouth.

"Please!" Magnificent Marvin cried out. "I still have several more shows tonight. That is the only cheese that Mikey likes. If I don't have it, then he won't do his tricks!"

As he bounded on to the stage Takahashi placed the piece of cheese on the stage in front of Mikey. Mikey sniffed at it nervously and then swallowed it in one big gulp. The crowd cheered for the obviously hungry mouse.

TEN

Magnificent Marvin groaned and smacked his forehead, knocking off his top hat as he did. When his top hat fell, a bird that had been hidden inside took flight. She flew right off into the night sky, surrounded by the shimmering lights of the carnival.

"Oh now you've done it!" Magnificent Marvin complained loudly. "That's it!" he screeched as Mouse came running up to the stage. "I'm done! I quit! I will never put on another show again!" he bellowed.

His audience began to disperse as Magnificent Marvin fell onto his knees and pounded on the wooden planks that the stage was made out of. He was not amused, not even a little bit, and Mouse realized that he was not going to take this as a joke.

Jaden, Amanda, Max and Rebekah had all gathered close. They were looking at each other nervously, wondering if they were going to get into big trouble for what they had done. But Mouse was staring forlornly at Magnificent Marvin.

Even though he had wanted to pull a prank on Marvin, even though he had hoped against hope that he would be able to trick Marvin, he had never wanted him to shut down his act.

Mouse had looked forward to it every year. Now he would never have the chance to see it again. Neither would the other kids that came out to the carnival, not just in his town, but in all the towns that the carnival visited.

He realized that his prank might have turned into a big problem instead of a big laugh. Magnificent Marvin did not look magnificent anymore. In fact, he didn't even look angry. He just looked sad. As sad as a man with a face full of glitter could look.

Mouse reached out and picked up Takahashi. He gently placed him into the box with Houdini and Magellan that Rebekah was holding.

ELEVEN

Rebekah shook her head slightly as she looked from Mouse to Marvin.

"We have to do something," she said quietly. "We can't let him shut down his whole act all because of our silly prank."

"I know," Mouse sighed and his shoulders drooped. He cleared his throat and walked up to Magnificent Marvin. "Excuse me. Mr. Magnificent Marvin?" Mouse asked as the man had finally discovered he had glitter on his face and was wiping it clean with a corner of his cape.

"You," he growled at Mouse. "Go on, get out of here! Haven't you done enough?" he demanded.

"Well, I just wanted to apologize," Mouse explained hesitantly. "I didn't mean to upset you."

"You didn't mean to upset me?" Marvin gasped as he looked at Mouse with disbelief. "This whole thing was planned. Upsetting me was your plan!"

"No it wasn't," Mouse said firmly. "I mean it," he added when Marvin shook his head. "It really wasn't. I love your show, and I just thought you would think it was all in good fun," he pointed out with a frown.

"Well I don't," Marvin snapped as he stood up from the stage. He picked up Mikey and placed him back into his silver maze box. "If you loved my show so much, why would you do this to me?" he asked with frustration.

"I just wanted to see if I could be good enough," Mouse explained. "If the idea my friends and I came up with would be good enough to fool you."

"Well congratulations," Marvin replied with a sigh. "You fooled me. You tricked me. You ruined Magnificent Marvin."

"I'm really sorry," Mouse said as his face fell. "I didn't mean to make you want to shut down your act."

"No matter what you meant, what's done is done," Marvin said firmly. "You've embarrassed me. There's no way I can go on again tonight or any other night."

"But you shouldn't be embarrassed," Mouse insisted. "I meant it to be a compliment. Because well, one day I hope to have an act like yours."

Marvin looked up at him with surprise. "You do?" he mumbled.

"Of course I do," Mouse grinned. "Who wouldn't want to have an act as amazing and dazzling as the Magnificent Marvin."

Marvin stared at him for a moment. He was trying to decide if Mouse was trying to trick him again.

"We're all really sorry," Rebekah added as she stepped up behind Mouse. "We really did think, since you play so many tricks, that you would think it was funny."

"Well," he paused a moment and glanced over the children before him. "It was pretty funny," he finally admitted. "I mean, the bit with the water and the glitter rag," he scowled at Amanda and Jaden. "That was genius," he admitted reluctantly.

"And whoever was responsible for the idea of being sent through the maze," Max raised his hand slightly. "Well young man, that was an excellent idea," Marvin laughed. "I got so dizzy in there that by the time I walked out I had to check to make sure there really was only one of me.

But, I still think it's time for me to retire. I mean, how could I even go on with another show after how embarrassed I am?" he shook his head and smiled sadly at the kids. "I know that you didn't mean it, but I'm going to get in a lot of trouble for this."

"But maybe you don't have to," Jaden suggested suddenly.

TWELVE

"What do you mean?" Marvin asked as he looked up at him hopefully. "Everyone saw it! The whole carnival will be talking about it!"

"Perfect!" Jaden smiled. "I think we can turn this into a great thing for you Magnificent Marvin."

"How?" Marvin asked skeptically.

"Yes, how?" Mouse asked with confusion as he looked at Jaden.

"All we need to do is make it all part of the show," Jaden explained with a shrug. "Sure everyone saw it happen, but what they didn't realize was that it was just part of the show."

"No one's going to believe that," Marvin huffed with a shake of his head. "They'll expect me to do the same show again, and when I don't, they'll know the truth."

"So..." Max said thoughtfully. "Do the show again," he smiled as he suggested this.

"What?" Marvin looked very confused.

"Max that's brilliant!" Amanda announced.

"Well it was Jaden's idea really," Max said with a shrug and a smile.

"What he means is, that you and Mouse should do the same routine again," Rebekah grinned as she explained this to Magnificent Marvin.

"Oh no way," Mouse shook his head and glanced away. "I'm sure that Magnificent Marvin would not want to share the stage with me."

Marvin was quiet for a few moments as he thought about the idea. "Actually," he finally said. "That's not a terrible idea. I think we could make it work," he smiled as he looked up at Mouse. "What do you think? Would you like to work the rest of the shows with me while we're in town?" he asked.

Mouse's eyes widened as he nodded his head quickly. He couldn't think of anything more amazing than sharing the stage with Marvin.

"I'd love to!" he said quickly. "I mean, if you really want me to."

"I do," Marvin assured him. "But we absolutely have to do that cheese bit again. That was hilarious!" he laughed as he remembered it.

"Of course," Mouse grinned.

THIRTEEN

That night, and for the rest of the weekend while the carnival was in town, Mouse got to star in Magnificent Marvin's show. Each time they did the routine of the mice running away with the cheese, it got the same sensational reaction. In fact, word spread quickly and each show was packed. Mouse was very proud to be part of the show. He was proud of his pet mice too, who were happy to play along. But most of all, he was glad that Magnificent Marvin had decided not to shut down his show. On the last night of the carnival Magnificent Marvin took Mouse aside.

"I want to thank you for doing the show with me," he said with a smile. He handed Mouse a special flyer he had made up. On it was his picture with Mouse beside him. The headline read: Magnificent Marvin, and underneath in the same bold writing was: Featuring Marvelous Mouse and his Marvelous Mice.

"This is fantastic!" Mouse said happily as he looked at the flyer. He planned to have it framed and hang it in his room.

"Next time I come to town, I hope that you will do the show with me again," Marvin smiled.

"I would be honored," Mouse replied with a proud nod. Even though his prank hadn't worked out exactly as he and his secret club had planned, it had still turned out to be an amazing adventure.

BOOK 5: PICNIC PRANK

ONE

It started out as a bright and sunny day. The sky was scattered with a few fluffy white clouds. The grass was green, the birds were singing. Mouse was sure that it was the perfect day for his picnic.

He couldn't wait to get to the tree house near the park. It was the meeting place for all of the kids in his secret club. They would get together at the tree house to talk about their plans for their next prank.

Mouse and his friends all enjoyed a good joke. Sometimes the jokes were on each other and sometimes they were on others, but they were always fun.

As he raced toward the tree house he held his hand lightly over the top pocket of his shirt. Inside his pocket was a small white mouse. It was one of Mouse's pets. Mouse had a collection of mice who were his pets, which is how he got his nickname, as he always had at least one of them with him. Today he had brought along Ferdinand, who was wiggling in his pocket.

When Mouse reached the tree house Rebekah and Amanda were already there. They waved to him from the small windows as he climbed up the ladder.

"So what's the big surprise?" Rebekah asked eagerly. Mouse had called them all together with the promise of a surprise but he refused to give the slightest hint about what it might be.

"Let's wait until everyone gets here," Mouse said as he sat down beside them inside of the large tree house.

"Aw," Rebekah pouted as she sat back. She didn't enjoy mysteries that she couldn't solve. Amanda crossed her arms and tapped her foot.

"I don't think I can wait that long!" she sighed.

"You won't have to wait long...look," Mouse said as he pointed out the window to the two other members of Mouse's Secret Club that were running toward the tree house.

Jaden and Max were laughing as they tried to beat each other to the ladder. Jaden won, as he was a fast runner. Max came in a close second. As they scrambled up the ladder Mouse stood up to greet them.

TWO

"Alright guys," Mouse grinned as Jaden and Max flopped down on the floor of the tree house out of breath from running. "In honor of what good club members you have all been, I'm going to have a special picnic for all of you today."

"A picnic?" Jaden asked with a raised eyebrow. He was still a little out of breath from running. "That's the surprise?"

"Sure," Mouse nodded, his smile wide as he took in the confused faces of his friends. "Doesn't that sound like fun?"

"I guess," Amanda shrugged, and then smiled. "Will there be decorations?" she asked hopefully. Amanda was a very good artist and loved anything that involved glitter.

"No decorations," Mouse shook his head. "Sorry Amanda."

Amanda's smile disappeared and she went back to crossing her arms.

"Will there be games?" Max asked hopefully. "I can have my Dad whip something up," he suggested. His Dad was a scientist and always had something new for Max to try out.

"No games," Mouse shook his head. "We're just going to have some good food and a good time." He was smiling very widely.

"Well what about a race?" Jaden suggested with a sparkle in his eyes. He knew he could win.

"It's just a picnic!" Mouse said and threw his hands up in the air. "That's it, nothing else. Just friends and food!"

"A picnic with a prank?" Rebekah asked slyly as she smirked at her good friend. "You're up to something, aren't you Mouse?"

"Be at the picnic tables by two o'clock this afternoon," Mouse said firmly. "Trust me, it's going to be great."

The way his eyes gleamed made all of the kids look at him funny. Rebekah nodded slowly.

'Yup he's definitely up to something," she giggled.

"Shh!" Mouse stomped his foot and glared at Rebekah. "No trying to figure it out. Just be there!"

"Alright, alright," Rebekah frowned. "No need to get so upset."

"Promise me Rebekah?" Mouse asked sternly. He knew how much she loved to solve any mystery she came across, and he was a little worried she would spoil his surprise.

"I promise," She sighed.

"Great, then I will see you all at the picnic tables at two o'clock!" Mouse declared. Mouse couldn't stop smiling, but his friends were all a little nervous.

THREE

Mouse was very excited for the picnic. He didn't usually plan things by himself as he liked to involve the whole club, but he wanted to surprise his friends with a special game. He didn't think they would enjoy it much, but he was sure it would be a lot of fun.

He went with his mom to the grocery store as soon as he left the tree house to get everything that he would need for the picnic.

As good as Mouse was at planning pranks he would get focused on one thing, and one thing only. He would never do something like check the weather forecast before he set out for his picnic. It just didn't seem important to him. The sky was blue after all, even if there were a few darker clouds creeping in.

So when he marched off toward the park with a picnic basket in one hand and a bag of supplies slung over his shoulder, he didn't even notice the sky getting more gray.

He arrived at the park earlier than his friends and began to set the picnic up. First he spread out the traditional red and white checked tablecloth. He even taped it down to make sure it wouldn't flutter off of the table.

Then there was the wicker picnic basket. He set it on the table and opened it up.

From inside he took out a small clear plastic cage and smiled at the little white mouse inside. He tossed a few bits of cheese into his pet's cage so that he would have something to munch on.

"Hi Ferdinand, at least you'll enjoy your meal," he grinned and set the cage on the table. Then he began pulling containers out of the picnic basket. He lined them up on the table one after the other and couldn't help giggling as he did.

Soon he heard his friends walking up to the picnic table. They were laughing and teasing each other about the picnic and what Mouse might be up to.

Mouse quickly pulled on a top hat and cape from the bag of supplies he had brought along with him. He even had a thin black cane to lean on. His friends looked at him oddly as they lined up in front of the picnic table. With his back to them he pulled out one more item to complete his costume.

FOUR

"Welcome, welcome," he said as he turned to face his friends with a fake bushy black mustache taped to his upper lip.

"Uh, Mouse," Max said as he tilted his head to the side. "You've got something-" he reached up and tapped on his own upper lip.

"Nonsense young man," Mouse barked and waved his hand toward the picnic table. "Please, take a seat, if you dare," he added with a wicked cackle that made Amanda's eyes widen.

"What is this about?" Rebekah asked suspiciously as she eyed the containers lined up on the table. She was a detective so she was suspicious by nature, and Mouse's costume made her even more suspicious.

"All will soon be revealed," Mouse promised in a thick accent that didn't sound like it belonged to any country.

"Oh dear it's worse than we thought," Amanda frowned as she shook her head. "Are you sure you're okay Mouse?"

"Who are you, and what have you done with our Mouse?" Jaden demanded as he scowled at Mouse and crossed his arms.

Mouse winked lightly from beneath the shadow of his top hat. "Never fear my friends, your Mouse is here! Because you are all so very special and unique, you have each been selected to be a part of a very special club. Today you will prove just how brave you are!"

"Uh oh," Rebekah sighed as she continued to study the large containers on the picnic. "This is one mysterious picnic."

"Marvelous picnic!" Mouse corrected with a huff. He gestured to the picnic table with his long thin cane. "Everyone, please take a seat!" he tapped the end of the cane on the bench of the picnic table.

Max, Jaden, Rebekah, and Amanda all gave each other worried looks. Knowing Mouse's excellent pranking skills they were all a little unsure about what would happen next.

FIVE

"Sit, sit," Mouse encouraged them and tapped the cane more loudly. Rebekah looked at Mouse, trying to figure out what exactly he was planning.

"Oh you four are not brave at all!" Mouse said in his strange accent. His mustache was starting to get a little loose. "That's it, you lose the game before it starts!" he announced with a grim frown.

"No wait!" Jaden cried out. "We're brave! We are!" Jaden insisted and sat down at the picnic table. Max sat down beside him, as he didn't want to be the last one to sit down. Amanda and Rebekah sat on the other side of the picnic table. Amanda scooted a little closer to Rebekah. They were all looking at the containers fearfully.

"We all know that a picnic is not complete without fantastic food!" he cackled and rubbed his hands together. Then he whisked off the top of the first large container. A strange scent wafted out of the container. It was spicy and strong.

"Our first treat has been scooped directly from the skull of a monkey," he announced in a growling voice. "Not just any monkey, but the rarest monkey in the entire jungle."

"Since when have you been to a jungle?" Rebekah asked with a skeptical frown.

"Hush!" Mouse insisted and snapped the end of his cane against the table right in front of Rebekah, making her jump at the sharp sound.

"Ugh!" Amanda shrieked and covered her eyes the moment she smelled the scent.

"Is that brains?" Jaden asked with horror as he peered inside of the container. "It looks like brains," he groaned.

Max couldn't say a word as he stared at the mush in the container with his mouth slightly open and his eyes wide.

"Some reward," Rebekah muttered with a shiver. Then she looked more closely at the contents of the container. "Hey wait that's just-" she started to say, but Mouse put his finger to his lips to quiet her and waved his wand in warning.

"Everyone take a bite!" he instructed as he handed out plastic spoons to each of his friends. He tried to hide his grin but he couldn't help but smile a little at their terrified faces.

"No, no, no," Amanda was chanting, she still had her eyes covered, so Mouse put her spoon down on the picnic table in front of her.

"I think I'm going to be sick," Jaden complained and shook his head. "I'll eat a lot of things, but brains is not one of them."

"Max?" Mouse asked as he held out a spoon to him. Max continued to stare. His face had gotten very pale.

"Really, no one?" Mouse asked with a frown. "This is only the first test!" he said with frustration that was made funnier by his thick and weird accent.

SIX

"I'll take a bite!" Rebekah volunteered with a smirk as she looked at Mouse. Max and Jaden stared at her with shock. Even Amanda peeked out from between her fingers at Rebekah with surprise.

"That's bravery!" Mouse said happily and pushed the container toward Rebekah. Rebekah picked up her spoon and grinned at her friends as she pushed it into the red and gooey contents of the bowl.

"Mmm," she murmured as she lifted a heaping spoonful toward her mouth. Amanda covered her eyes again.

"No, no, don't do it," she shrieked and whimpered at the same time.

Jaden and Max leaned forward watching as Rebekah opened her mouth. Rebekah popped the entire spoonful into her mouth and grinned as she chewed it up.

"Yum!" she declared when she had swallowed the spoonful.

Max looked like he might fall over. Jaden was staring at the mush in the bowl. Amanda was whimpering quite loudly now.

"Can I have some more?" Rebekah asked cheerfully and smacked her lips as if it was delicious.

"Aw Rebekah you're ruining it!" Mouse complained as he took off his top hat and tossed it on the table.

"What?" Rebekah asked innocently as she looked at him and shrugged. "I can't help it if I happen to like monkey brains."

"Who could like monkey brains?" Jaden demanded, his eyes as big as saucers.

"Who doesn't?" Rebekah giggled. "Try it Jaden," she winked at him and pushed the bowl toward him. He stared at her with confusion and horror.

"Is Rebekah the only one brave enough?" Mouse asked as he put his hat back on the top of his head and straightened out his mustache.

"Yes!" Amanda announced and cringed as she caught another whiff of the strange scent that wafted out of the container.

The wind was beginning to pick up, and it seemed to be blowing the smell right in her direction. Max was still only staring silently. When Rebekah jostled the container and the monkey brains slid back and forth with a slosh, he groaned and looked away.

"No," Jaden said sternly as he picked up his spoon. "If Rebekah can try a bite, then so can I," he said with a nod. He jabbed his spoon into the monkey brains. When the spoon squished into it he grimaced.

"Oh, maybe I was wrong," he mumbled and started to pull his spoon back out.

"Just try it," Rebekah encouraged him. "It's really tasty. Just don't think about where it came from," she tried not to giggle as Mouse shot her a look.

"Okay," Jaden sighed and scooped up a small spoonful of the monkey brains. Just as Jaden was about to take a bite, a big roll of thunder carried through the sky. It got everyone's attention.

SEVEN

"Oh no!" Mouse cried out as he looked up at the sky with surprise, losing his strange accent. "It's not going to rain is it?" he gasped.

"Didn't you see the weather forecast today?" Max asked, finally finding his voice again. "We're in for thunderstorms all afternoon!" he shook his head as he stared up at the sky. "Looks like a mean one to me."

"Oh no," Mouse sighed with disappointment. "Well hopefully we'll have a few minutes to-" before he could finish his sentence the rain began to pour down. It filled up the bowl of monkey brains. Mouse scrambled to cover it up, but when he did, he accidentally knocked over the plastic cage that Ferdinand was in.

"Mouse! Your mouse!" Amanda squeaked as she pointed to the white blur scrambling through the grass.

Mouse lunged after Ferdinand hoping to catch him before he got too far away. But his foot slipped on the already slick grass, and he went tumbling head over heels. He landed hard on the ground that was getting very muddy.

"Ouch," he groaned. Max snatched up the plastic cage and chased after Ferdinand while Rebekah ran to Mouse's side.

"Are you okay?" she asked him as she helped him up off of the ground.

"I think so," he said as he sighed. He looked up at the sky and the rain drops struck his face. "Some picnic," he huffed.

EIGHT

Every time Max got close to Ferdinand the little mouse managed to escape. Once Max had the cage just about on top of him, when he slid across the slick grass and the mouse bolted away.

Jaden tried to catch him as he was running the other direction, but Ferdinand wanted nothing to do with being caught. He seemed to like the rain, and splashing through the puddles that were growing. He ended up running right back under the picnic table. He ran right over Amanda's feet.

"AH!" she cried out and jumped up from the picnic table. As she did she tripped on the bench and grabbed the tablecloth to try to stop herself from falling. Instead the tablecloth ripped off of the table, and pulled along with it were the containers of food that Mouse wanted them to try.

Monkey brains splattered everywhere, along with ogre eyeballs, and a few gobs of slimy snake guts which landed squarely on Amanda's shirt.

"Oh no! Oh no!" she cried as she danced around trying to wipe the guts off without actually touching it. Jaden came to her rescue with some rain soaked napkins.

Mouse watched as the chaos unfolded. His plan for a great prank picnic had surely not included a thunderstorm. Ferdinand had gotten caught under the tablecloth so Max was finally able to trap him in the cage.

"Look, I got him," Max said happily as he brought the cage back to Mouse with Ferdinand inside. The poor mouse was soaking wet and shivering.

NINE

"Thanks Max," Mouse said happily though his smile was not very bright. "I guess that's it everybody. We'll just have to go home," he looked sadly at the food that had been dumped all over the ground and the ripped tablecloth.

"Yes!" Amanda said with a squeal of joy. "That means I don't have to eat any of the monkey brains!"

"It was just spaghetti and sauce," Rebekah giggled as she helped Mouse clean up the containers that were scattered all over the ground. "And peeled grapes?" she guessed as she picked up one of the ogre eyeballs. Mouse sighed and nodded as he scooped up what was left of the snake guts.

"And marshmallow peanut butter goo," he added.

"Really?" Amanda gasped with surprise. "I love spaghetti! And grapes! And peanut butter and marshmallow!" she sighed with disappointment. "Great, now I'm hungry!" she grumbled and ran off through the rain. Rebekah met Mouse's eyes over the picnic table. She could tell that he was very disappointed.

"It was a good idea Mouse," she said with a smirk. "And some of the best prank picnic food I've ever seen."

"I couldn't even fool you," Mouse sighed as he picked up the last of the items that he had brought along to the picnic.

"Don't worry about it Mouse, we still had fun," Rebekah assured him as she helped him fold up the tablecloth.

"I'm going home to dry off!" Jaden called out as he ran off across the grass.

"Me too!" Max shouted as a loud roll of thunder sounded above their heads.

Mouse waved as the two ran off leaving only Rebekah and Mouse soaking up the raindrops. Mouse didn't even seem to notice the rain. There was no way Rebekah was going to leave her friend behind, no matter how hard it was raining. As they walked back across the grass with picnic supplies tucked under their arms, Mouse sighed again.

"Maybe I'm not the best president for this club," he mumbled under his breath. "Maybe this whole club was a bad idea," he added gloomily.

"Mouse don't be silly," Rebekah shook her head. "This club is the most fun part of my week!"

"Maybe," Mouse shrugged a little but he still couldn't manage a smile. "But I can't even host a simple prank picnic," he pointed out and walked off toward his house.

TEN

When he got home he marched right into his room. He didn't even change his wet clothes. He just put Ferdinand into the big cage with his mouse friends and then plopped down on his bed.

He stared at the ceiling sadly. He had no idea how long he was laying there, but it wasn't until his phone started ringing that he realized his clothes were dry. He picked up the phone to discover that it was Rebekah calling.

"Hi Mouse," she said far too cheerfully.

"Hi Rebekah," he sighed.

"Do you think we could have a special meeting of the club tomorrow?" she asked.

"What club?" he sighed.

"Oh Mouse, don't be so dramatic," Rebekah insisted. "Please can we have a meeting tomorrow?" she asked.

"I guess," Mouse sighed. "Maybe we could elect a new leader of the club."

"Only if we can find another Mouse," Rebekah said happily.

"Sure," Mouse sighed again and hung up the phone. Mouse was so upset over his failed prank that he couldn't sleep all night. He kept thinking if he had just checked the weather forecast, if he had just thought it through and made sure that he was prepared, his prank would have worked out just fine. Instead he had ruined the whole prank.

By the time the sun came up the next day he was ready to give up his club altogether. It had been fun while it lasted. But how could he claim to be the leader of a club that created pranks if he couldn't even pull off his own.

He still didn't want to disappoint Rebekah though, so he made himself get up out of bed. He made himself eat a little breakfast. He made himself walk down toward the park. But he dragged his feet the whole time.

When he reached the park he noticed that none of his friends were around. He was sure it was because they were so embarrassed by his failed prank the day before.

ELEVEN

Mouse climbed up the ladder to the tree house. He was surprised when he saw all of his friends were already there. He was also surprised when he saw the small table was covered with a picnic blanket.

"Surprise!" Rebekah cried out happily and clapped her hands. On the table were three large containers.

"Welcome to a picnic just for you Mouse!" Rebekah announced with a grin. Jaden and Max were all smiles as well. Amanda was holding her nose, but she was smiling too.

"What is this?" Mouse asked with confusion as he sat down at the small table.

"Well the weather forecast said we might get another storm today," Max explained with a shrug. "So we thought we better take the picnic inside."

"You guys did all this for me?" Mouse laughed.

"We thought your picnic prank was great," Amanda explained. Her voice sounded very strange since she was still holding her nose. "So we thought we'd do it again. Only this time, you're the one that gets the spoon," she handed him a large plastic spoon. Mouse took the spoon and eyed the containers nervously.

"Thanks guys," he said and raised an eyebrow. "I think." Mouse was pretty sure he was in trouble.

"This is a gourmet food," Amanda explained as she lifted the lid off of one of the containers. "It's called raw worms a la dirt," she giggled as Mouse looked down at the dish before him. He studied it for a moment, while all of his friends watched him stare.

"Mm," he grinned and picked up a spoon. He could see the worms mixed into the dirt, but that didn't stop him from digging right in. He took a big bite of the dirt, and made sure there was a worm in it too.

"How can you just eat that?" Jaden laughed and shook his head. "You're one brave Mouse!"

"Mm, tastes like chocolate and gummy worms," Mouse grinned as he chewed up the bite of food.

"Well you might like that one," Max said with crossed arms as he glowered at Mouse. "But this one you'll never touch," he opened up the next container. Inside were what looked like long green legs. They were even a little stringy. Mouse turned his head sideways. He looked very closely at the food in the container. Then he tried to hide a smile.

"Oh tasty," Mouse cheered and snatched up one of the legs. He crunched right into it, and chewed it up quickly. Max stared in horror as he crunched away.

"You would eat frog legs?" he asked with absolute surprise.

"No," Mouse laughed and shook his head. "But I would eat celery, and that is very fresh celery," he said with a grin. He picked up another leg and crunched right into it.

"Oh give it up," Jaden groaned and threw up his hands. "He's never going to be fooled. How could we even think we had a chance against the master of pranks?"

Mouse blushed at that. He couldn't help but grin. After spending the night and morning thinking he wasn't worthy of being the leader of the club, he was now seeing that his friends all seemed to think otherwise.

TWELVE

"We'll see about that," Rebekah said with determination as she opened up the last container on the table. "I made this one, and no one knows what it is," she added with a sly grin.

"I know it is the stinky one!" Amanda declared as she pinched her nose again and backed away from the container.

"You know I have to say on this one she's right," Jaden agreed as he backed away from the table too. Even Max took two steps back, and bumped right into the wall of the tree house.

Mouse stayed right in front of the table. He wasn't looking at the container, he was looking at Rebekah, who was still smiling very smugly.

"Alright Mouse, here's your chance to show us just how brave you are," she giggled as she met his eyes.

Mouse narrowed his eyes and looked down at the dish. It was wiggly, and it looked very strange. He wasn't sure what to think of it. It didn't look like anything that he had ever seen before. Still he took the spoon that Rebekah handed him, ready to dive in.

"Is it spaghetti?" he asked curiously as he poked at the long strands that looked like legs.

"Nope, not spaghetti," Rebekah giggled with glee and pushed the container closer to him. "Go on, just try a little Mouse."

"Huh," Mouse poked the dish some more and looked up at her. "Is it some kind of stringy beef?" he asked.

"Nope, not beef at all," Rebekah replied and clapped her hands with delight. She was certain that for once she was fooling Mouse. "No more guessing!" she said sternly. "Just take a bite and munch away!"

Mouse was starting to get a little worried. He had guessed that the worms and dirt were chocolate and candy by the sweet smell. He had guessed that the frog legs were celery because of how stringy they were. But this food was something he couldn't quite figure out.

Something about it seemed familiar, but he wasn't sure why. He leaned in close and breathed in the scent of it. He realized right away that this was a terrible mistake. The awful smell that filled his nostrils made his stomach churn.

"Uh, Rebekah, are you sure about this?" he asked and glanced up at her nervously. "It didn't go bad or something on the way to the tree house?" he wondered.

"Nope, it's quite fresh," Rebekah laughed loudly. "My Mom and I picked it up at the store today."

Mouse was a little relieved by that. At least he knew that it was something that he could buy at the store.

"What is it?" he finally asked, knowing she wouldn't tell him the truth.

"It's octopus," Rebekah replied proudly. "I think if you take a bite, you might just like it."

"Octopus?" Mouse asked with a grin. "Ha, ha, Rebekah, very funny," he poked at the food again. He had to admit it did look a little bit like octopus. "Go on take a bite," Rebekah said again. "I already cut it into little pieces for you. Show us all how brave you are!" she said with an evil grin.

"Oh whatever Rebekah," Mouse rolled his eyes scooped up a bite of the food and then stuck the spoon right into his mouth.

When he closed his mouth over it, he expected it to be jello, or something else familiar. Instead it tasted kind of rubbery and slimy. His eyes widened as he looked at Rebekah.

THIRTEEN

"Rebekah?" he asked around the food in his mouth. "Is this really octopus?" he asked, his eyes growing even bigger.

"Well I said it was, didn't I?" Rebekah squealed with laughter. Mouse was so surprised that he accidentally swallowed the octopus.

"Ugh! Ack!" he grabbed at his throat and stuck out his tongue. "Yuck! Rebekah, how could you?" he glared at her.

"I told you what it was!" Rebekah pointed out around her laughter. Her friends were all staring at her with horror. They had no idea it was really octopus either. "I thought and thought about what is the best way to fool the best prankster in the world. Then I realized, it's not to fool him at all! Instead of lying, I told you the truth."

"Why?" he demanded as he guzzled down a bottle of water that was on the table. "Why would you do this to me?" he moaned.

"Oh Mouse," Rebekah rolled her eyes. "Don't be so dramatic, again. I knew I didn't need to prove to everyone else how brave you are, I just needed to prove it to you.

You were brave enough to take a bite of that octopus, just like you are brave enough to think up the best pranks! You are the only Mouse that could ever lead Mouse's Secret Club!"

Mouse sighed as he finished the bottle of water. He looked around at his friends and felt much better than he had the day before. In fact he felt downright mischievous.

"Well good," he said with a smirk. "First order of club business, everyone has to try some octopus!"

"No!" Amanda shrieked and headed down the ladder of the tree house. Jaden and Max were right behind her with Rebekah impatiently waiting her turn. Mouse laughed as he watched his friends scramble as far and as fast from the tree house as they could.

BOOK 6: FUN HOUSE

ONE

"Okay class we are going to have a special competition," Mr. Burke said as he walked away from the chalkboard. "We want to raise money for some new sports equipment.

We wanted to try something a little different. Instead of selling candy or cookies or candles, we thought we'd ask for your ideas for fundraisers."

Mouse perked up at that. He had been looking out the window and daydreaming. He had already finished his work and was just waiting for the bell to ring. When he heard the words special competition, he began paying close attention.

"The rules are simple," Mr. Burke continued as he walked back and forth in front of the first row of desks. "You have to come up with an idea for a fundraiser.

You can come up with it on your own, or you can work together with a group. The idea has to be new, nothing done before like a car wash or a bake sale.

We want to see how creative you can be," he added with a smile. "It can't be just an idea though, we expect you to provide us with a plan. You'll make a list of all the supplies you'll need, when and where you would hold the fundraiser and why you think it should win the competition."

Mouse's mind was already spinning. He was sure that this was the perfect project for his secret club. The club was a group of his friends who all enjoyed a good prank. They worked together to come up with the best ideas they could for fun pranks to play, so he was sure that they could come up with something great for the competition. The boy sitting beside Mouse raised his hand.

"Yes?" Mr. Burke asked.

"What do we win?" the boy asked with an eager smile. Mouse hadn't even wondered what the prize would be.

"Well if you win we will use your idea for the fundraiser," Mr. Burke explained. "And you will get a gift card to the hardware store."

"Hardware?" one of the kids in the back of the class groaned. "Who would want that?"

Mouse's eyes were huge. He would want that. He could already think of millions of pranks he could create with so many supplies. He opened up his notebook and began jotting down his ideas.

TWO

As soon as the bell rang he began hunting down the other members of his club in the hallways. He found Max trying to cram his entire collection of chemistry books into his locker. They weren't even for school, but he loved to learn anything about science.

"Need some help?" Mouse asked as he helped shove the books into the locker.

"Thanks," Max sighed with relief as he managed to close the locker door all the way before it could pop back open.

"Listen we need to have a meeting after school, okay?" Mouse asked. The club met in a tree house they had found in the woods beside the park.

"I'll be there," Max promised and waved as he hurried down the hall. Mouse nearly ran into Amanda who was walking backwards as she unfurled a streamer that was connected to the top corner of her locker.

"What are you doing?" Mouse laughed as he managed to avoid crashing into her.

"Just a little decorating," Amanda replied and ripped off the end of the streamer. Then she taped the light pink paper to the front of her locker. It did make her locker look much more festive.

"Good job," Mouse nodded with approval. "Meeting today after school, okay?" he smiled.

"I'll be there Mouse," she promised and taped down another streamer. Mouse knew he only had a few minutes left between classes. He was searching for Jaden and Rebekah as he hurried down the hall.

"Jaden!" Mouse froze when he heard Jaden's name shouted down the hallway by a very upset teacher. "No soccer in school!"

Then Mouse spotted Jaden kicking the ball right down the middle of the hallway.

"Sorry Mrs. Cooper!" Jaden called back over his shoulder as he chased down the soccer ball. Mouse stopped it with his foot and reached down to pick it up.

"Here you go Jaden," he said and handed it to him.

"Thanks Mouse," Jaden sighed with relief. "It just got away from me."

"I know the feeling," Mouse said as he tucked a small white mouse back into the top pocket of his shirt. Mouse always had one of his many pet mice with him. That was how he got his nickname, Mouse. But many times his pet would escape. He was trying to be more careful with them. "We're having a club meeting after school, okay?" he asked.

"I'll be there," Jaden promised and bounced the soccer ball once on the floor.

"Jaden!" Mrs. Cooper hollered.

"Sorry!" Jaden cringed. "I better get this in my locker," he grinned and jogged down the hallway toward his locker. Mouse was just about to his next class when he spotted Rebekah staring at something taped on to the wall.

"Hi Rebekah!" Mouse called out as he hurried over to her.

"Hi Mouse," Rebekah said in a distracted voice. "I think this would be perfect for the club!" she announced as she pointed to the poster on the wall that was all about the fundraiser contest.

"How do you always do that?" Mouse asked as he laughed.

"Do what?" Rebekah asked with surprise.

"I was just coming to tell you about that, but as usual you figured it out first," he grinned and shook his head.

"Well, I am a detective," Rebekah explained with pride in her voice.

"Good point," Mouse nodded. "So we'll meet up at the tree house after school?" he asked hopefully.

"Sure thing," Rebekah nodded as the bell rang. "I know we'll win!"

Mouse was pretty sure they would too as he walked off to his class.

THREE

After school they were all gathered together in the tree house. Everyone was shouting out ideas at the same time.

"An arts and crafts booth!" Amanda suggested.

"A murder mystery!" Rebekah cried out.

"An obstacle course!" Jaden said as he waved his hand in the air.

"How about a guess that element game?" Max said happily, which made everyone stop and look at him. Max was one of the smartest kids around and the fact that his father was a scientist made it even worse.

"No elements?" he asked with a half smile.

"It has to be something new and different," Mouse said thoughtfully. "Those are all good ideas, but they've been done before. Well, maybe not the murder mystery, but I don't think the principal is going to let us murder anyone even if we're pretending!"

"Good point," Rebekah sighed.

"And the element game might be fun for you Max, but I don't think everyone would enjoy it," Mouse offered with a frown.

"I guess you're right," Max nodded. "We need something that's going to be fun, fun, fun for everyone!"

Max's words made Mouse remember something. He had visited the circus over the summer and there were some special shows after. He remembered a clown on stilts shouting that same thing: Fun, fun, fun for everyone! The clown had been advertising a fun house.

"That's it!" Mouse snapped his fingers. "We could have our own fun house!"

"Fun house?" Jaden asked and shook his head. "What's that?"

"It's like a haunted house, only fun," Rebekah explained with a growing smile.

"I don't like haunted houses," Amanda said sternly. "No way."

"It's not a haunted house," Mouse insisted. "It's a house full of tricks and pranks. What could be better for us?" he asked with a grin.

"That sounds like a great idea," Max agreed with a quick nod. "I've been to one before and it was a little scary but mostly just fun."

"I think if we work together we could come up with some great little pranks to go inside the fun house," Mouse pointed out. "We could build it in my backyard," he added.

"Well, as long as it's not too scary," Amanda finally agreed.

"We have to make plans to give to Mr. Burke," Mouse explained as he pulled out a notebook. "So let's figure out how we can do this."

"Well, we would raise the money by selling tickets to the fun house, right?" Jaden asked.

"Sure," Rebekah nodded. "I think all the kids at school would want to go, and they would probably get their parents to buy tickets too. It could make a lot more money than any old car wash or bake sale."

"Then I won't have to bring my own soccer ball to school," Jaden laughed.

As they worked together on outlining their project and the ideas they had for it, the sun slowly began to set. By the time they were done, they had been working for a few hours.

"Wow!" Mouse said as he looked outside to see the sky getting dark. "We better get home. We can meet up before our first class tomorrow and turn this in to Mr. Burke," Mouse suggested.

"See you then!" Rebekah called out as she climbed down the ladder.

Max followed her, his eyes glowing with ideas of all the tricks he could come up with.

Amanda was excited because she was going to be in charge of designing the fun house and painting it.

Jaden was dreaming about a new soccer ball and other sports equipment.

Mouse was sure that their project would be chosen. He was so happy that he nearly skipped all the way home.

FOUR

The next morning Mouse and his friends gathered together outside of Mr. Burke's classroom. They were about twenty minutes early for school, so Mr. Burke was still getting prepared for his first class.

"So are we sure we have everything straight?" Mouse asked as he looked over the information they had written out the day before.

"Looks good," Rebekah nodded and patted Mouse's shoulder. "It's going to work!"

"Needs one thing," Amanda said and sprinkled a little bit of glitter on the paper.

"Amanda!" Max groaned. "Mr. Burke isn't going to be impressed by glitter."

"You never know," Amanda said with a smirk.

"Alright, let's give it a shot," Jaden said as he tilted his head toward the classroom door that Mr. Burke had just opened.

"Mr. Burke?" Mouse called out before the door was even all the way open.

"Mouse," Mr. Burke smiled. "You're here early, is there something I can help you with?"

"Yes," Mouse held out the paper. "We have an idea for the fundraiser."

"Already?" Mr. Burke asked with surprise. "Well that's fast work kids," he took the piece of paper and scrunched up his nose as a few specks of glitter tickled his hand. "Looks like you put a lot of work in here," he said with interest as he looked over the information.

"Do you think it might win?" Mouse asked eagerly. Mr. Burke read over the paper again. He stared at it for a long time and then looked up at Mouse and his friends, who were waiting for his answer.

"To be honest with you Mouse, no I don't," he said with a frown.

Mouse hadn't been expecting that answer. He thought maybe Mr. Burke would say that it had a good chance. He thought maybe he would say that Mouse would just have to wait and see like everyone else. But he didn't expect to be told that their idea had no chance.

"But why?" Mouse managed to ask, though his eyes were still very wide.

"Look, I think it's great," Mr. Burke explained calmly. "But we're looking for something uplifting, inspiring. Not something like a haunted house. That will just be too scary."

"But it's not a haunted house," Rebekah insisted with narrowed eyes. "It's a fun house!"

"Well, it's kind of the same thing," Mr. Burke explained with a shrug. "Listen, the only reason I'm telling you this is that you will have time to come up with another idea. I love how you all worked together as a team to create this. So just work together to create something a little different."

"But it's a great idea," Jaden pointed out. "Everyone would enjoy it!"

"I know that you all think it is great," he said patiently. "But the principal and the teachers have the final say. I'm sure they're not going to want to do this. I'm sorry," he added as he looked back at Mouse. "But don't let it stop you from getting together and creating another wonderful idea."

As Mr. Burke stepped back into the classroom, Mouse couldn't hide his disappointment. He shook his head as he turned back to his friends.

"I'm sorry guys," he said quietly. "I guess it wasn't the best idea."

"It is the best idea," Rebekah said confidently. "We all think so. Don't we?" she asked as she looked at each of her friend's faces. Jaden, Amanda and Max all nodded. Everyone was disappointed that Mr. Burke hadn't even considered their idea.

"Thanks," Mouse sighed. "I just wish that Mr. Burke had understood. It's not a haunted house, it's a fun house."

"Sometimes people just don't get an idea until they see it," Jaden shrugged and then glanced up as the bell rang. "See you later!" he called out and ran down the hall. Mouse sighed and headed toward his classroom, as did Jaden, Amanda and Rebekah.

FIVE

Mouse could barely pay attention in his classes. He kept looking down at the paper filled with plans for the fun house. He was sure that it would be great. He was sure that Mr. Burke would like it if he just gave it a chance.

Then he thought about what Jaden had said about some people not getting the idea unless they saw it. He snapped his fingers in the middle of class. The teacher shushed him.

"Sorry," Mouse mumbled and sank down in his chair. He wasn't disappointed anymore. Now he was determined. He was going to make sure that their idea had a chance. When school was over he caught up with Rebekah. He was out of breath by the time he ran up to her.

"I think we should do it!" he gasped out.

"Do what?" Rebekah asked with surprise. "Are you okay?"

"Yes. I think we should build the fun house!" he said quickly.

"What? Why?" Rebekah frowned with confusion. "Mr. Burke already said no to the idea."

"He did, but that's because he doesn't understand our idea!" Mouse explained as he fell into step beside her. "We just need to show it to him. So if we build the fun house, then he will be able to see it in person and I bet he will change his mind!"

"I don't know," Rebekah shook her head slowly. "Adults can be pretty stubborn."

"And so can I," Mouse replied as he crossed his arms.

"Well that's for sure," Rebekah laughed and then nodded. "I think it's a good idea Mouse. Even if it doesn't change Mr. Burke's mind, we can still have fun with it."

"Great!" Mouse clapped his hands sharply. "Then we'll get started this afternoon. Do me a favor and call Amanda, Max and Jaden for me. I have to convince my Mom that the backyard should be off limits while we build this."

"Good luck," Rebekah grinned, and then ran off toward her house.

SIX

When Mouse walked in the door his mother was looking through a magazine as she waited for him.

"Mouse!" she said happily when he walked in. "How did it go?" she smiled. Mouse had showed her the plans that he and his friends had come up with because he was so proud of their idea.

"Not well," Mouse admitted with a sigh.

"Why not?" his mother asked as she stood up and walked over to him.

"I just don't think Mr. Burke understands what we're trying to do," Mouse explained as he set his book bag down. "But we were hoping to still build it anyway. So is it okay if we use the backyard for a few weeks?"

"How exactly do you plan to use it?" his mother asked suspiciously. She had gotten used to some of Mouse's pranks and they did not always end well.

"Just to build the fun house," Mouse explained quickly. "We don't want anyone to see it until it's done."

"Alright, as long as you promise to be careful," his mother hugged him gently. "I'm sorry your idea didn't get chosen," she added.

"There's still time to change Mr. Burke's mind," Mouse said with a determination. He was sure that if anybody could pull this off, it would be him and his friends. Within an hour the entire club was out in his backyard, buzzing with excitement.

"I can't believe we're still going to build it!" Amanda said happily.

"It's a great idea," Max agreed as he smiled at Mouse.

"Think of it his way," Jaden suggested. "Even if we don't change Mr. Burke's mind, we could have our very own fundraiser and still donate the money to the school."

"That's a fantastic idea," Rebekah nodded and high-fived Jaden. "Let's do this!" she cheered. The other kids did as well, everyone but Mouse, who was already clearing out his workspace. He was so determined that he didn't want to take the time to celebrate.

SEVEN

Mouse's backyard became a construction zone. The members of the secret club were in and out of the yard with the supplies they were able to find.

Amanda gathered some funky reflective paper from her art supplies. She also found some ribbon with odd fuzzy dots on it.

Jaden was able to get some boards and other lumber from his father's workshop.

Max had purchased some very brightly colored paint and had a bottle of his father's homemade glow in the dark formula.

Rebekah had several different sized magnifying glasses and she also had a noise device that made very different loud sounds.

Mouse had all the tools from hammers and nails to sandpaper to smooth the edges of the wood.

The group met every day after school to put the fun house together. Mouse knew that the principal still might not agree to use it for the fundraiser, but they were having so much fun building it together that no one seemed to care.

It took them almost two weeks to build, but when they were

putting the final touches on the fun house everyone was proud of their work.

"It looks fantastic," Mouse said as he took a step back to look at it. The outside was painted with bright yellows and blinding oranges. There were two fake windows on the front with eyes that seemed to be peering out at them.

Amanda had even drawn a clown on stilts on the front of the fun house There was a rainbow colored windmill on the roof of the house. When the wind spun it, it made loud whistling sounds. It really was great.

EIGHT

To celebrate Mouse's mother ordered them all pizza. As Mouse and his friends were digging into extra cheese slices, they were all smiles. But Mouse was still a little worried.

The fun house was done and it looked great, but would Mr. Burke think so? And how were they even going to get Mr. Burke to see it? When they had finished their pizza and everyone was about ready to head home Mouse walked them to the door.

"Listen guys, phase one is complete. But we need to come up with a way to get Mr. Burke, the principal and as many teachers as we can to come here to see the fun house," he pointed out.

"We could just haul it to school somehow," Jaden suggested.

"No," Mouse shook his head. "If we got in trouble for it they might keep the fun house. I don't want to risk that."

"Me either," Amanda agreed. Max looked thoughtful as he rubbed his chin.

"Well, we could always pretend we're having a meeting of some kind," he said slowly.

"Sure," Rebekah nodded. "We could tell them that we're having a barbeque!" she said with a clap of her hands. "To honor all their hard work. Then when they get here, no barbeque, just a fun house!"

"Great!" Mouse laughed.

"They might be angry though," Jaden pointed out nervously.

"And hungry," Amanda added with a frown.

"Well then we'll make sure we actually have a barbeque," Mouse's mother said with a smile as she walked up behind the group of kids. "It's not a good idea to lie to your teachers guys. But if we really do have a barbeque and there just happens to be a fun house as well, well then that would work, wouldn't it?" she grinned.

Rebekah looked up at Mouse's mother with a huge smile. "I see where you get it from Mouse!"

Mouse laughed and nodded. "I think this is going to work!"

"I know it will," Rebekah promised.

That night when Mouse lay down to go to sleep, he could barely keep his eyes closed. He was so excited to show off the fun house, and he hoped that it would be chosen as the winner of the competition.

NINE

When Mouse arrived at school the next day some of his excitement had faded. He was worried that Mr. Burke and the other teachers wouldn't agree to come to the barbeque. He wondered what he would do if he said no.

As if he knew that something was wrong, a little pink nose poked up out of Mouse's pocket. Mouse smiled at his pet. He had the pinkest nose of all of his mice, so his name was Bozo.

He always had a way of cheering Mouse up when he was feeling down. Mouse patted him on the top of his head and then tucked him back into his pocket.

"You're right Bozo," he said as he headed for his locker. "We just have to hope it will work."

When he reached his locker and was working on opening it, someone walked up behind him and shouted "Surprise!"

Mouse gasped and jumped as he spun around to find Amanda standing behind him with a huge grin.

"Wow you got me!" he laughed and shook his head.

"Look what I made," Amanda said as she held out a stack of envelopes.

"What are these?" Mouse asked as he looked through them. Each one had a different teacher's name on it.

"They're invitations," she explained. "To hand out to the teachers. I thought it might make them more likely to agree to go."

"Excellent!" Mouse nodded as he shook the envelopes a little. He could hear something moving around inside. "Let me guess, glitter?" he asked.

"Well, they wouldn't be invitations without glitter now, would they?" Amanda giggled and hurried off to her class.

"Thanks Amanda!" Mouse called after her. He dropped off as many invitations with teachers as he could before his first class. Then between each class he dropped off more.

When he got to Mr. Burke's class, he only had his invitation and the principal's invitation left.

"Hi Mr. Burke," Mouse said as he walked in.

"Hi Mouse," he smiled. "I hope you're not too upset with me."

"No I'm not," Mouse promised him. "Here," he handed him one of the invitations. "My friends and I are hosting a teacher appreciation barbeque this Saturday. We'd like you to be there."

"How nice!" Mr. Burke said with a smile. "Count me in," he added as he opened the envelope. Unfortunately he opened it upside down and ended up with a pile of glitter on his grade book.

"Amanda," he sighed and shook his head.

"Amanda," Mouse agreed with a short laugh as he walked to his desk.

TEN

On the day of the barbeque Mouse was nervous. He and his friends had gone through the fun house to make sure that everything was in working order.

Some of the teachers he had invited had said they were coming, but there was no way to know for sure. The weather looked beautiful and Mouse's mother had purchased everything they needed for the barbeque.

Rebekah and Amanda were helping her put all the food out while Jaden was filling a cooler with ice and Max was bringing the meat out from inside the house to cook. It was going to be a great day, even if all the teachers refused to go inside the fun house.

Mouse couldn't help but be nervous though. Bozo was nervous too as he wiggled around inside Mouse's pocket.

"Don't worry," Rebekah told him when he paced by her for what seemed like the hundredth time. "It's going to go great!"

Mouse nodded, but he could barely smile. His stomach was churning, his heart was racing and Bozo was doing flips inside of his pocket. When Mr. Burke arrived Mouse breathed a sigh of relief. He led Mr. Burke out to the back yard.

"What a nice home you have," Mr. Burke said politely and set down the bag of chips he had brought for the party. "This is so thoughtful of you and your friends and-" he stopped in the middle of his sentence and looked at the fun house right in front of him. The fun house with a large clown painted on the front.

"Wh-what is that?" he asked nervously.

"Oh we decided to make the fun house after all," Mouse explained quickly. "Would you like to see inside?" he asked hopefully.

"No, no, no I would not!" Mr. Burke backed away so fast that he nearly bumped into two other teachers who had just arrived.

"Oh dear," Ms. Sonya sighed when she saw the clown painted on the outside of the fun house. "Mr. Burke is a little frightened by clowns," she explained to Mouse in a whisper.

"I'm not frightened by them," Mr. Burke said sternly. "I just prefer not to be around those big red noses!" he squeaked and hurried over to the table.

"Oh no," Mouse moaned as he joined his friends. "Mr. Burke isn't going to go inside the fun house if he's afraid of clowns!"

"Well, we'll just have to show him that they're not so scary," Rebekah suggested with a grin.

"How are we going to do that?" Mouse asked and shook his head. "I don't think this is going to work."

"Yes it will," Max said firmly. "I know just how we can do it! I'll be back in a flash!" he shouted as he ran out of Mouse's back yard.

ELEVEN

Soon the rest of the teachers had arrived. No one seemed interested in going into the fun house.

Mouse looked at his watch and wondered what Max could be up to as he had been gone for so long. Then he noticed something very strange. A very tall clown was walking into his back yard. It was a clown on stilts, just like the one they had painted on to the front of the fun house.

"Hi everyone!" the clown called out, in Max's voice.

"Max?" Rebekah gasped as she looked way up at the clown.

"Clown!" Mr. Burke shrieked and jumped up from the table. He started running toward the house, but Max walked in front of the house. So Mr. Burke ran the other way.

A few other teachers ran after him to try to get him to calm down. Mr. Burke was in such a panic to get away from the clown that he ran right into the fun house. Mouse ran in after him, trying not to laugh too loud.

As soon as Mr. Burke stepped into the fun house, the windmill on the roof began to whistle. The walls glowed with weird shapes thanks to the glow in the dark paint.

The floor shook and rumbled thanks to the sheets of metal they had put underneath of it. Mr. Burke hurried down the hallway that led to the next section of the fun house.

Here there were three bubble machines. As soon as he stepped inside they all started shooting bubbles off until the room was filled with them. Mr. Burke and the two other teachers with them were covered in bubbles.

"Ugh!" one of the teachers said.

"I love bubbles!" the other teacher said and began trying to catch some.

"Clown!" Mr. Burke said and hurried out of the room. With their clothes and skin covered in bubbles the next room was sure to tickle them because it had four fans that blew feathers into the air. The feathers stuck to their skin and clothes because of the bubbles.

Both of the teachers with Mr. Burke had to laugh at this. Mouse was struggling to keep up with them as Mr. Burke was moving through the fun house so quickly.

When he stepped into the next section of the fun house the lights flickered and flashed. Strange sounds filled the room, from the roars of tigers to the bleating of sheep.

Mr. Burke spun around as he heard each sound. He nearly fell over one of the other teachers. As Mouse lunged in to help him keep his balance, Bozo slipped right out of his pocket. Mouse didn't notice as his pet scampered into the next room.

When Mr. Burke had his balance he hurried into the next room. This room was the mirror room. They had combined the reflective paper with Rebekah's magnifying glasses, making the mirrors reflect some strange and funny images. Mr. Burke was halfway through the room when he suddenly stopped short.

TWELVE

"What is that?" he gasped as he looked in the reflective paper. The two teachers behind him skidded to a stop.

"Mouse!" one of the teachers shouted.

"Clown!" Mr. Burke shouted.

"Bozo!" Mouse shouted as he saw the huge dark pink nose reflected all over the room. As the teachers ran out of the last room and Mouse struggled to catch Bozo, the entire fun house started to shake.

All the shoving and scrambling was too much for the flimsy structure and it was beginning to wobble. Mouse snatched up Bozo and ran out of the fun house just before it began to collapse.

"Oh no!" Rebekah cried out. All of Mouse's friends gathered around him as the structure they had worked so hard on began to crumble.

"So sorry Mouse," Amanda said softly. Mouse tucked Bozo back into his pocket. He tried to hide how sad he was. Worse than that, he was sure that Mr. Burke was going to be furious. Max had climbed down off of his stilts and taken off his big hair and red nose.

Mr. Burke was leaning on the picnic table gasping for breath.

Mouse thought it was because he was so frightened, or maybe because he was so angry but as he stepped closer to Mr. Burke he discovered it was because he was laughing so hard that he couldn't make a sound.

"Mr. Burke?" Mouse asked nervously.

"That was by far the funniest thing I've seen in a long time!" he said as he laughed. He pointed at the two other teachers who were picking feathers off of their clothes. "You were right Mouse. Your fun house is perfect for the fundraiser!"

Mouse was surprised. "But I thought you were afraid of clowns," he said.

"Sometimes it takes confronting your fear to realize how silly it is," Mr. Burke said as he continued to laugh. "You five have won the competition. You can use your gift card to rebuild the fun house. It's going to be the best fundraiser ever!"

Mouse and his friends cheered. Max tried to hug Mr. Burke, but he backed away quickly.

"Okay, okay clowns might be funny, but not too close!" he said with a squeak, which made everyone at the barbeque laugh.

BOOK 7: IT'S A BIRD!

ONE

Mouse looked at the large brown package in his living room and rubbed his hands together. He was very excited. His grandfather had sent him a special gift.

His grandfather tended to forget birthdays and holidays as he was always traveling. But Mouse never minded that because when his grandfather sent a gift for no reason at all, it was always the best gift ever.

He was so excited about it that he almost didn't want to open it. He had been staring at the box ever since he got home from school. It was getting close to dinner time and he decided he was finally ready to open it.

When he tore the tape he was careful. He liked to keep the boxes his grandfather sent because they usually had some interesting post-marks and stamps on them.

As he opened the box he held his breath wondering what would be inside. He pulled away some bubble wrap and found two fierce eyes staring up at him. He jumped a little as they looked so real, glassy and dark as they looked up at him.

It took him a moment to realize that they were attached to a dark blue material. Carefully he lifted the gift out of the box. It wasn't until he had it all spread out that he realized what it was.

It was a kite, but it looked nothing like a kite. In fact, it looked like an animal. The eyes were raised and made out of a very light plastic. The kite had wings that moved separately from the rest of the body of the kite. Mouse was sure that they would look like they were flapping when the kite flew through the air.

It was nothing like any kite he had ever seen before.

"Mouse, what did grandpa send?" his mother called from the kitchen as she was getting dinner ready to put on the table.

"Uh, just some books this time," Mouse called back. He wasn't sure why, but he wanted to keep his gift a secret this time.

His mind was already spinning with a prank he might be able to play with it. He placed it carefully back into the box and carried it quickly into his room. Once there he found the note his grandfather had packed in the box with it.

"In the tiny village where I am staying making kites is a favorite hobby. I asked one of my friends in the village to make this for you. I hope that you like it. Sorry he couldn't make a Mouse!"

Mouse grinned at the note and at the idea of a kite shaped like a mouse. That would be a pretty interesting kite. He made sure that the door to his bedroom was locked then he pulled the kite out again.

He laid it across his bed. It was big and very lifelike. Of course anyone looking at it would know it was a kite but with a few touch ups and some sound effects, Mouse was sure that his idea was going to work.

First he would run it by his friends, all members of his secret club to make sure that they thought so too. He put the kite away again and began making calls to set up a club meeting after school the next day.

Mouse and his friends had a special club that came up with the best pranks ever. They met in a tree house that they found in the woods just outside the local park. Mouse was sure that his friends were going to love the idea too.

TWO

When Mouse met up with his friends at the tree house they were all curious about what his new plan might be. Mouse had his new kite hidden under a sheet as he climbed up to the tree house. He laid it out on the table in the middle of the tree house.

"What's that?" Rebekah asked as she tried to peek under the sheet.

"It's what we're going to use to make the whole town believe there's a new bird flying around," Mouse laughed as he pulled back the sheet to reveal the kite.

"Wow that's amazing," Amanda said as she moved one of the wings carefully.

"Have you flown it yet?" Jaden wondered.

"Look at those eyes!" Max exclaimed as he stared at the glassy eyes.

"I haven't flown it yet," Mouse admitted. "My grandfather sent it to me from whatever country he's exploring right now. I think it's great, but it made me realize we could play a great prank on the town."

"What prank are we going to play?" Rebekah asked, her eyes shining with the idea.

"Well, with wings and eyes like it has, I think it could be mistaken for a real bird," Mouse explained as he sat down in front of the kite.

"That's true," Max nodded as he narrowed his eyes. "But people would only mistake it for a bird when they first see it. Once they looked closer they'd see it was a kite."

"You're right," Mouse agreed. "Unless we make it look even more like a bird," he grinned.

"How are we going to do that?" Jaden asked.

"Oh I know how!" Amanda clapped her hands. "We could add feathers. They're light enough that the kite can still fly, but they will make the kite look more like a bird."

"Exactly," Mouse grinned. "And if we add in some sound effects to make it sound like the bird is tweeting, then we'll really fool everyone."

"We're really going to need your talents on this one Amanda," Mouse said as he looked at her. Amanda couldn't stop smiling.

"I'll bring all my art supplies," she said happily. "I can already picture it in my head. This is going to look like a real bird."

"A giant bird," Jaden pointed out with a laugh. "I bet someone will think it's prehistoric."

"It's going to be great," Rebekah nodded as she glanced over at Max. "Do you think we can work together to create some sounds that sound like a real bird?"

"Sure," Max nodded. "I have a new program on my computer that lets me work with all kinds of sounds and change how they sound. You can come over tomorrow after school and we can work on it," he suggested.

"It's a plan," Rebekah smiled.

"Okay so Amanda, Jaden and I will meet at the tree house tomorrow and work on the bird, while you and Max work on the sound effects," Mouse smiled. "We're going to have the whole town going wild with this."

THREE

Rebekah and Max sat down at his computer desk in his room. His room was filled with everything science. There were planets hanging from his ceiling and a chemistry set was set up across his other desk.

His bookshelves were overflowing with all kinds of books. He had all of the latest gadgets and actually knew how to use them, which was more than Rebekah could figure out. On his walls he had posters with different constellations and some with endangered animals on them.

Max had already opened the program he had on his computer that would help them come up with a new sound for the bird. They were playing different sounds when Max's father stuck his head into the room.

"What are you two up to?" he asked with a grin as he had heard the strange sounds from the hallway.

"It's just a project for school Dad," Max explained. Max's father was a scientist and he and Max were always working on projects together.

"Well let me know if you need any help," he said cheerfully before he walked away.

"Your Dad's nice," Rebekah said with a smile.

"He is," Max agreed. "But if he found out what we were up to, I don't think he'd be too happy about it. He doesn't understand why pranks are fun."

"Really?" Rebekah asked with surprise.

"Nope, not at all," Mouse laughed. "I once shook his hand with a buzzer in my hand, and he spent an hour explaining to me how the buzzer worked instead of just laughing."

"Wow," Rebekah giggled. "We better hope he doesn't find out then."

"Absolutely," Max grinned and then pressed play on the sound they had created. It sounded like a mix between the caw of a crow and the tweet of a song bird. It was odd, and loud and perfect.

"Wait until Mouse hears this!" Rebekah said gleefully.

They toyed with the sound just a little more so that it would have background noises with it, like the sound of the wind and the trees rustling. Then they saved it on to an old MP3 player Max had hung on to.

"This won't be too heavy to put in the kite," he said as he tested the weight in his hand. "And we can set the sound on repeat."

FOUR

Meanwhile in the tree house, Mouse, Jaden and Amanda were hauling all of Amanda's supplies up the rope ladder.

"Do you really need all of this?" Jaden asked with a huff as he set down a box of paints inside the tree house.

"Well an artist is never sure of what she'll use until she gets to work," Amanda explained with a smile.

"Well I can tell you it sure is a lot of work to get all these supplies up here," Jaden pointed out and flopped down in a chair. The kite was spread out across the table and Mouse was looking at it very closely.

"In order for this to work we're going to have to fill out the body of the bird a little more, so it doesn't look so flat," Mouse said thoughtfully.

"Well lucky for you, I brought cotton balls," Amanda said happily and showed him the bag of cotton. "I think they'll work well to fill out the bird, and they will be light enough that the bird will still fly."

"So what kind of feathers are we going to use?" Jaden asked as he peered into the large plastic bag crammed with feathers that Amanda had brought along.

"Well since the kite is a dark color I was thinking of using dark feathers too," Amanda explained. "So how about a blue bird?" she suggested.

"Blue sounds great," Mouse nodded and then looked right at Amanda. "But no glitter!"

"Well some birds wings are so shiny they seem to shimmer-" Amanda began to protest.

"No way," Jaden shook his head. "Mouse is right. We want the bird to look real and if you put glitter on it, people are going to figure out it's fake right away."

"Alright fine," Amanda sighed and tucked her glitter away. Mouse and Jaden worked together to stuff and tape cotton ball into the kite so that it would look more lifelike. When they were finished the bird looked pretty good.

"Alright Amanda," Mouse said as he looked over at her sorting through her supplies. "Can you turn this kite into a real bird?" he asked.

"Absolutely!" she replied with confidence. Then she pulled out her glue and began to make careful dots along the surface of the kite. She placed dark blue feathers on each dot, so that they overlapped. She made sure that some of the feathers covered the crease of the wings. By the time she was done gluing the feathers, the kite really did look and feel just like a bird.

"Wow," Mouse shook his head. "It's better than I thought it would be!"

"It could be sparkly," Amanda reminded them as she capped her glue.

"No sparkles," Jaden and Mouse both said, then all three laughed.

"Wow, that looks real!" Max said as he climbed up into the tree house. Rebekah was right behind him.

"You did a great job," she said as she admired the kite that now looked just like a bird.

"Listen to this," Max smiled proudly and played the sound that he and Rebekah had created together.

"Wow!" Jaden grinned. "That's spooky."

"And loud," Amanda groaned and covered her ears.

"It's perfect," Mouse said with confidence. "Now we just have to hope that our little bird will fly. We should try it at night," he added. "That way no one will spot it until we're ready to let them see it."

"Tomorrow night?" Rebekah suggested. "We can try it out in the open field by the swing set."

"Tomorrow night," Mouse agreed.

FIVE

Getting through school the next day was very hard for Mouse. He didn't think he was ever going to be able to wait until the sun set to try out the kite. He had checked on it that morning to find that the feathers were dry. It looked very much like a real very large bird.

He was excited to see how well it would fly in the sky. Would it look real from the ground? Would the sound make it come alive?

He could barely focus on his work in class, but he still did his best.

After school he headed over to Rebekah's to discuss the plans for their meeting that night.

Before he did he scooped up one of his favorite pet mice, Wilbur. Wilbur had been one of Mouse's pets for quite some time. Mouse got his nickname from all of the pet mice he owned. He almost always had one or more of them along for a ride in his pocket. Usually it wasn't Wilbur though.

Wilbur was very wiggly and didn't like to stay still for very long. But it had been a while since he had been out and about and Mouse thought he could use some fresh air. Still, on the walk to Rebekah's house he had to tuck Wilbur back into his pocket three times to keep him from crawling out. Finally he tossed a few bits of cheese into his pocket to keep Wilbur busy.

Rebekah was waiting for him when he walked up the driveway.

"I wish it was night right now!" Rebekah grumbled as she held open the door for him.

"Me too," Mouse admitted. "Let's just make sure we have everything that we need for tonight and hopefully the time will pass by fast."

As they went over a checklist of items, Mouse's other friends began arriving. Everyone was restless and eager to get out into the field.

"Okay so we'll meet right after dinner," Mouse said sternly. "Don't be late, because we have to be back home before curfew. So we'll only have about an hour to try this out."

Everyone agreed to be there, and on time.

SIX

Mouse scarfed down his dinner, barely taking a breath between bites. His parents stared at him strangely.

"Mouse are you okay?" his mother asked as she watched him shovel in another forkful of food.

"Mmhm, it's just so good," he mumbled around his bites of food.

"It's meatloaf," his mother pointed out with a raised eyebrow. Meatloaf was not one of Mouse's favorite meals.

"Just hungry I guess," Mouse shrugged as he wiped his mouth with a napkin. "May I be excused?" he asked.

"I suppose," his mother nodded.

"Going out?" his father asked as Mouse grabbed his jacket.

"Yes, I won't be out long!" Mouse called back over his shoulder.

"What could he be up to that he's in that much of a hurry?" his father wondered.

"Sometimes dear, it's better not to know," Mouse's mother smiled.

When Mouse reached the clearing his friends were already there. Jaden and Max had already carried the kite down from the tree house and it was sitting on the grass. Mouse was surprised to see it. It really did look like a bird.

"Wow, I can't wait to see it in the sky," he said happily.

It was very dark, but there were plenty of stars in the sky. Mouse laid the kite down on the ground in the middle of the clearing very carefully.

"I brought some fishing twine that will be invisible," Mouse explained as he handed Jaden the roll. Jaden tied it on to the kite and then spread out the fishing twine far enough that it would give Mouse a good running start.

Amanda was standing by with glue and feathers in case any fell off during the flight.

Rebekah had a camera to film the entire flight. She thought they could use the video to tell if the flight looked like a real bird.

Max was checking the volume on the MP3 player. He made sure it was loud enough to be heard. Then he slipped it inside the kite. Once he was sure it was taped securely inside, he turned the sound on. He had left a small delay at the beginning of the loop so that the kite would have time to get into the air.

Mouse looked over the kite one more time, then smiled with a nod.

"I think it's ready," he said proudly. All of his friends stood together as he began running down the field toward the other side.

Once the kite got up into the air, he held it steady. Rebekah ran over to him and grabbed the end of the fishing line. She tied it around the small remote control car. She made sure the string was tied nice and snug.

Then she nodded to Mouse. Mouse let go of the line, and the kite continued to float in the air. Jaden had the remote control and began to drive the car across the field. As he did, the kite flew through the sky.

The fishing line was invisible, so it really did look like a bird flying through the air. Its wings flapped. Its feathers fluttered. Soon it was letting out its unique cry.

"It works!" Mouse jumped up and down and threw a punch of celebration into the air.

"It looks so real," Amanda gasped as the bird swooped in the wind.

"We're going to fool everyone," Max said with a grin. Jaden steered the car back toward them.

"Let's get it down before it gets stuck in a tree," Jaden laughed.

Mouse pulled it carefully down to a soft landing. As they put away the remote control car and covered the kite up with a sheet again, they were all very excited about the next day.

SEVEN

When Mouse woke up and ran to the kitchen for breakfast the next morning his Mom had the news on.

"So what was that in the sky?" the reporter was asking. Mouse barely noticed until he heard the reporter talk about a bird.

"We're fairly certain it was a bird," an expert was explaining to the reporter. "But from its size, its coloring, and its call, we're not sure what kind of bird."

"Interesting," the reporter said. "Do you think it's anything our local citizens should be concerned about?" she asked.

Mouse stared at the screen, his mouth full of eggs as it hung open.

"Not just yet," the expert replied and looked into the camera. "But if it is a new species like we suspect, then we need to find out what it is and how it got here."

"Ew Mouse close your mouth!" his mother complained when she turned around to see his mouth hanging open. "Interesting about this strange bird, isn't it?" she asked.

Mouse had wanted to surprise the people of the town, but he certainly hadn't expected it to become breaking news. Could they really be talking about his bird?

"Interesting," Mouse nodded and then closed his mouth.

EIGHT

When he arrived at school all of the kids were talking about the strange bird that had been spotted. There were lots of theories as to what it might be. Mouse noticed Max walking into school with his head hanging pretty low.

"What's wrong Max?" Mouse asked when he walked up to him. "Didn't you see the news?" Mouse grinned proudly.

"Yeah I saw it alright," Max replied and frowned. "So did my Dad. Now he's calling all of his scientist buddies. He wants to see if they can catch it so they can study it."

"Oh no," Mouse frowned. "Don't worry, this will all blow over," he promised Max.

"I hope so," Max said with a sigh. "I don't want my Dad to think I was trying to trick him."

"Don't worry about it," Mouse said and patted his shoulder. "We'll make sure that the kite is put away and everyone will forget about the bird."

But by the end of the school day there had been even more news reports about it. Some people in town had taken pictures and video of the kite flying. All of the videos and pictures had been submitted to the news stations.

There was a lot of talk of the town becoming a protected area if the new species of bird was found.

Mouse knew that things were spinning out of control and just hoped that a few days without the kite flying would make people lose interest.

NINE

He hurried to the park after school and climbed up into the tree house to get the kite. But when he looked inside, the kite was gone!

"Oh no!" Mouse cried out.

"What's wrong?" Rebekah called from below the tree house. She, Jaden and Amanda were looking up at him. They had heard about the news stories and wanted to make sure the kite was safe and put away.

"It's gone!" Mouse climbed back down the ladder. "It's nowhere in the tree house!"

"But where could it be?" Rebekah wondered as she looked up at the tree house. She was already trying to solve the mystery.

"Maybe Max has it," Jaden said as he glanced around. "He's the only one who isn't here."

"No look," Amanda said as she pointed across the park to the other side of the clearing. "There he is."

Max was standing at the edge of the clearing looking up at the sky.

"Max!" Mouse shouted to him. "What are you doing?"

Max was still staring up at the sky. He slowly raised his hand into the air and pointed at something. Mouse, Rebekah, Jaden and Amanda looked up at the sky. What they saw was not something that they expected.

Soaring above them with its wings flapping in the air was the bird! It was out in the middle of the day for everyone to see!

"Ugh!" Mouse gasped. "How could that have happened?" he demanded.

"It was windy while we are at school," Amanda pointed out. "Maybe it blew out of the window of the tree house!"

"But how is it flying?" Mouse asked as Max jogged over to him.

"I don't think this is my idea of keeping things under wraps," Max said with a frown. "I'm sure the whole town is seeing this."

"I'm sorry Max," Mouse shook his head. "I don't know how this happened."

"It doesn't matter how it happened," Jaden said with a growl. "But we need to figure out how to get it down!"

"Well if it's flying it has to be attached to something," Rebekah pointed out. "Remember we can't see the fishing line, so it must be stuck to something."

They began searching over the tree house for any sign of the fishing line. Max finally found the roll of fishing line stuck to one of the branches that held up the tree house.

"Here it is!" he announced. He began winding up the line as fast as he could. The bird bucked in the sky, then swooped down quickly, just as a news van was pulling into the parking lot of the park.

"Hide it quick!" Mouse said and grabbed the sheet they had been hiding it under. By the time they had it under wraps, a reporter and camera man were running across the clearing.

"Kids, kids, did you see it?" the reporter asked and shoved a microphone toward them. "Did you see the bird?"

"Uh, I didn't see anything," Max stammered.

"None of us did," Mouse said firmly.

"Isn't it pretty though?" Amanda grinned into the camera. She had made the bird after all.

"It's very pretty," the reporter agreed. "If we could only figure out where its nest is!"

"Well it looked like it might be flying south for the winter," Mouse pointed out with a shrug.

"But it's spring," the reporter said.

"Maybe it's confused," Rebekah smiled into the camera. "Even birds get lost you know."

"Maybe," the reporter smiled and turned to look into the camera. "We missed the bird again, but it can't hide forever!"

"It sure can't," Max muttered under his breath.

"I think we're going to have to come clean on this one," Mouse frowned grimly.

TEN

When Max arrived at home he found his father and two of his scientist friends waiting for him.

"Max, we just saw you on television!" Max's father said with a grin. "Did you see the bird?"

Max stared at his father. He wasn't sure what to say.

"I uh," Max shifted from one foot to the other. "I did see it," he admitted.

"Well, did you see where it landed?" one of the men beside his father asked eagerly. "Do you think you could help us find its nest?"

"I don't know," Max looked down at his shoes.

"Well why don't we go take a look," Max's father suggested.

"That would probably be best," Max nodded. He knew that Mouse and his friends were waiting at the park. When Max reached the park with his father and his friends, Mouse and the rest of the secret club were hiding behind the bushes.

"Okay here he comes," Rebekah whispered. "Get the bird ready."

Mouse leaned over the kite and checked the fishing line. He didn't notice when something slipped out of his pocket.

"Ready?" Jaden asked as he turned on the remote control. He had the other end of the fishing line tied to the car.

"Ready," Mouse agreed. Jaden made the car drive fast behind the bushes. The kite flew right up into the sky.

"There it is!" the tallest scientist shouted as he pointed up into the sky. "Would you look at that!" he cried out and pulled out his cell phone to record the bird flying through the air.

"It's amazing," the short scientist said with a shake of his head.

"To think my son Max led us right to it," Max's father said and clapped his son on the shoulder. Max smiled a little and shot a look over at Mouse that said 'Help me'.

Mouse knew that now things had gone too far. It was one thing for it to be on the news, but now there were real scientists investigating the bird. Someone was going to figure out it was a hoax sooner or later.

Mouse didn't want Max to get in trouble with his father for playing such a prank. He looked over at Rebekah, who looked over at Jaden who nodded at Amanda. They all knew that they were going to have to tell the truth before things got any messier than they were.

ELEVEN

Jaden steered the car that was hidden by the bushes until it was driving right in front of the scientists. But they were looking up at the sky, not at their feet. They didn't notice the remote control car until it bumped into the tallest scientist's shoes.

"What's this?" he gasped. He crouched down and picked up the car. When he picked it up he noticed the fishing line tied to it. "Hm," he said and gave the line a tug. When he did, the kite began to come down closer to the ground.

"Look, it's going to land!" the short scientist said and pointed at the sky.

"Oh it's going to land alright," the tall scientist said as he stood up and began pulling harder on the fishing line.

"Max what is going on here?" his father asked as the kite plummeted to the ground.

"Dad, I can explain," Max started to say.

"Actually Mr. Harper, I can explain," Mouse said as he walked up to him. The kite landed in the grass not far from them.

"That's not really a bird," Mouse sighed as he looked over at the kite. "We just made it look like it was."

"Hm," the short scientist said. "You mean our rare bird is a fraud?"

"Yes," Rebekah admitted as she stepped up beside Mouse. Jaden held up the remote control that controlled the car as he walked up. Amanda pointed out the feathers on the kite.

"I did a pretty good job with the wings huh?" she smiled charmingly.

The scientists were silent, including Max's father. Mouse was nervous that they were going to get very angry.

"Tell me this young man," the short scientist said as he looked sternly at Mouse. "If that's not a real bird, then why is it still moving?" he asked.

TWELVE

Mouse looked over at the kite in time to see it scampering across the grass.

"Huh?" Mouse asked with surprise.

"Mouse the kite is getting away!" Rebekah shrieked.

"Catch it!" Mouse cried out. "I don't want to lose it!"

Max, Mouse, Rebekah, Amanda and Jaden all began chasing it across the field, with the scientists watching.

The kite ran straight for the scientists. Before Mouse could catch up with it, it had bumped into their shoes. Max's Dad crouched down to grab a hold of it.

Even after he grabbed the wings, the kite continued to wiggle as if it was trying to get away. When Mouse skidded to a stop beside it, Max's Dad was inspecting it closely.

"Well, well," he said with a slow smile. "It may be that we missed out on spotting a rare bird, but I think we've found an even more rare animal."

"What?" Max asked with surprise as he looked at his father. Mouse and Rebekah looked at each other and then at Jaden and Amanda. They had no idea what Max's father was talking about.

"It looks like we have found our very first flying mouse," Max's dad said proudly as he pulled a little white mouse out of the inside of the kite.

"Wilbur!" Mouse said with surprise. "How did you get in there?" he huffed as Max's father handed him the mouse.

"Looks like he wanted to try some wings on," he said with a chuckle.

"You're not mad Dad?" Max asked nervously.

"Mad?" his father shook his head. "Not really. I'm sure we're all a little disappointed," he said as he glanced at his friends. The two men nodded. But the tallest one smiled.

"But the fact that all of you were able to pull all of this off, and fool even us, just goes to show that the new generation really does love science!" he laughed.

"I'm expecting to see good things from you in the future young man," the short scientist said and patted Max on the head.

BOOK 8: MOUSE NINJA!

ONE

Mouse woke up with an idea. He had a dream about being a ninja. It was a lot of fun to be dressed in all black and sneaking around. When he woke up, the dream about being a ninja made him think of a perfect prank to play on his friends.

Mouse had his very own club, a secret club...Mouse's Secret Club to be exact. His friends were members of this club. Together they would plan out the best pranks ever.

Usually they worked as a team, but sometimes Mouse liked to play a prank all by himself. His dream about being a ninja made him think of a perfect ninja prank.

When Mouse arrived at school, he was ready to start his prank. It had been quite some time since he played a prank on the members of his club and he was betting they wouldn't even suspect him. This time he was going to make it a good one.

In one pocket he had a bottle of green goo. In the pocket on his shirt, he had his pet mouse Marty. Marty was a very curious mouse. He was always poking his nose up out of Mouse's pocket. He didn't try to escape; he just wanted to see everything that was happening around him.

As Mouse walked down the hallway, Marty's little nose poked up out of his pocket. The halls were filled with kids trying to get to their lockers and back to class on time.

Mouse was the only one who didn't seem to be in a hurry. That was because he already had permission to be late to his first class. Mr. Cooper had agreed to it so that Mouse could pick up a stack of books from the library that his students were going to begin reading.

Mouse scanned the kids for his friends. He noticed a few of them and did his best to avoid them. He didn't want them to see him before school started. He smiled as the bell rang.

Once the hallways were clear, Mouse crept up to his best friend Rebekah's locker. Rebekah was a great detective and Mouse loved playing pranks on her to see if she could figure out who had done it. This made her the best first target. Plus, he knew her locker combination which was helpful.

Once he had her locker open, he snatched her history book off of the top shelf of her locker. It was her heaviest book and she didn't like having to carry it around all day, so she always put it in the same place in her locker.

He stuck it inside of his backpack. Then he coated the shelf with green goo. He tried not to laugh as he expected she would think an alien or a very slimy green slug had invaded the school. She would never suspect a Mouse ninja.

He hurried down the hall with her history book hidden in his backpack. He skidded to a stop in front of one of the empty classrooms and disappeared inside of it.

A few moments later he ducked back out and headed down the hall to collect the books from the library and return them to Mr. Cooper's class. He was feeling very confident about his trick as he walked into the classroom.

"Good job Mouse," Mr. Cooper said as he took the stack of books. "Uck, what's this?" he asked when he pointed to a smear of green goo on one of the books.

"Sorry," Mouse said and wiped it with the corner of his shirt.

"Oh Mouse," Mr. Cooper sighed and shook his head. Mouse grinned and took his seat.

TWO

After class Mouse was on the hunt for his next victim. He knew all of his friends' schedules. His next target was Jaden.

Jaden was a hard one to prank because he was always moving. Even when he was standing still he was usually tapping his foot or slapping his hand against his leg. Most of the time he had some kind of ball to kick or toss. He was in a lot of sports to try to burn off some of that energy.

Jaden was scheduled for gym at the same time as Mouse's math class. Mouse was a whiz at math. He could add, subtract and multiply with his eyes closed. Okay, so could most of the other kids in his class, but he was still very good at math.

He finished his assignment very quickly and then raised his hand.

"Mrs. Barkley can I have a bathroom pass?" Mouse asked with a squeak in his voice to make it sound like an emergency. Since he was already done with his assignment, Mrs. Barkley gave him the pass.

"Hurry back," she said sternly. "No roaming the halls!"

Mouse nodded and walked quickly out of the room. As soon as he was outside in the hall he broke into a run. It was against the rules to run in school, but since he had a bathroom pass most of the hall monitors looked the other way.

Mouse ran all the way to the bathroom and then he took a hard left and headed for the gym. He slipped inside when no one was looking and hid behind the bleachers.

Jaden was in the gym with his friends. He had his shoe on his soccer ball so that he could tie the laces. Mouse watched from behind the bleachers. He waited until Jaden put his foot down. Then he rolled a basketball out into the middle of the gym from behind the bleachers.

When Jaden saw the ball rolling, he couldn't resist. He snatched it up and dribbled it over to the basketball hoop to take a shot. Quick as a flash Mouse jumped out from behind the bleachers and grabbed Jaden's soccer ball. He left behind a few drips of green goo where the ball had been.

Once Jaden made his shot he turned and ran back to get his soccer ball. Of course now it was nowhere to be seen. Jaden was confused as he reached the spot where it had been.

"Anyone take my ball?" he asked as he looked around the gym at his friends. No one had it. Jaden turned back and as he did, he stepped right into the green goo. His foot slipped and slid in the goo.

"Ah!" he cried out as he lost his balance and ended up landing right on his bottom on the hard gym floor. "Ouch," he grumbled. But as he stood up he discovered something much worse, he had landed right in the pile of goo.

His gym shorts were covered in green goo! Mouse tried not to laugh from where he was hiding behind the bleachers. He hadn't meant for Jaden's shorts to get messy, but it was pretty funny and they were just his gym shorts. Jaden sighed and trudged into the locker room to change.

While he was gone, Mouse slipped out of the gym and ran back to his class. When he stepped inside his classroom the teacher was just getting up to look for him.

"Sorry it took so long Mrs. Barkley," Mouse said as he handed her back the pass. Mrs. Barkley nodded and directed him back to his seat.

Mouse tried to hide his grin as he sat down in his chair. He was sure that Jaden was searching for his soccer ball.

After Jaden had changed he went back into the gym to look for his soccer ball.

"It couldn't have just disappeared," he frowned as he looked where he had seen the ball last. "I know I left it right here."

He crouched down to take a closer look at the green goo that was on the floor.

"How strange," he muttered and shook his head. He was sure that someone or something had taken his ball and he was determined to find out who it had been.

"Jaden, why aren't you in your gym shorts?" Ms. Vincenzo his gym teacher asked.

"I slipped in some goo," Jaden tried to explain but the look on Ms. Vincenzo's face made him realize she wasn't going to understand. "Someone stole my soccer ball," he added with a frown.

"I'm sure it just got put away with the other sports equipment," Ms. Vincenzo shrugged. "You can look after class."

"Okay," Jaden nodded sadly. But even after class when he searched the equipment closet, he didn't find his soccer ball.

THREE

Mouse had lunch for his next period class, but he wasn't interested in eating. He ducked into the lunch room long enough to get counted as present and then slipped right back out.

He had brought with him the perfect tool to get Amanda's attention. He knew where she would be, since they shared a lunch period, but she never actually showed up for lunch.

This time he had to be careful in the hallway. He had no pass to be wandering around and the hall monitors were much stricter during lunch hours.

He made his way carefully through the halls, ducking into doorways whenever he heard footsteps. He didn't want to get caught because then his prank spree might be over!

When he reached the art room he breathed a sigh of relief.

Amanda was humming to herself as she put together a collage in art class. She had stayed later than the rest of the kids as she liked to spend her lunch period working on her art projects.

She was alone in the classroom when Mouse peeked around the door. He smiled to himself and knew just how to get Amanda out of the room. He reached into his pocket and pulled out a bottle of glitter. The bottle was tied to a piece of string.

He rolled the bottle into the art classroom and crouched down just outside. Luckily it struck the table where Amanda was working. She gasped with surprise and looked down at the bottle.

"Weird," she mumbled and reached down to pick it up. Mouse gave the string a little jerk and the bottle rolled away from Amanda.

"Hey get back here!" Amanda demanded and stood up to chase it. Mouse gave the string another tug and the glitter bottle rolled all the way out into the hall. Before Amanda could reach the door, he flung the glitter bottle down the hall away from the classroom door.

"Ugh!" she chased after the bottle of glitter.

Mouse ducked into the classroom. He knew he had to work fast. Marty stuck his nose up out of Mouse's pocket. Mouse grabbed Amanda's go-to-glue. It was a special bottle of glue that she always had with her and she saved for her most important projects. He dribbled some of the green goo on the desk next to her art project.

As he was turning around to run out of the room, Marty slipped out of his pocket. Mouse snatched him up and tucked him back into his pocket before he could get away.

He hurried out of the room just as Amanda was turning around to walk back to the art classroom. He ducked around the corner before she could spot him.

"We did good Marty!" Mouse said happily as he patted the top of his pet's head. Marty wiggled his nose and then ducked back into Mouse's pocket.

When Amanda walked back into the classroom with the bottle of glitter, she was pretty confused.

"Maybe I kicked it," she mumbled to herself and set the bottle of glitter on to the shelf of supplies. When she sat back down at her desk she sighed and looked over her collage.

It was a collection of pictures and mementos from all the pranks she and the other members of Mouse's Secret Club had played. No one else would know what they all meant, but she thought it would look great in the tree house where they held their club meetings.

She picked up the picture she wanted to add next and reached for her special bottle of glue. But she only found air.

Surprised she searched the table. She looked under the piles of pictures and other art supplies, but it wasn't there. She looked under the table, but it wasn't there either. When she put her hand down on the table, she felt something strange.

"Ew," she gasped as she picked up her hand to find green goo all over her palm. There was something else too and it looked like little footprints. She had no idea what could steal her glue and leave behind a trail of goo and tiny footprints.

"Maybe an alien elf?" she thought and scratched her head. Then she realized she had just scratched her head with the hand covered in green goo. "Ew!" she cried out again and grabbed some paper towels to clean her hand and hair.

FOUR

Mouse made it back to the lunch room just in time to grab an apple. He collapsed into a chair and sighed. All of this ninja work was making him pretty tired. But he knew it was going to pay off in the end. It was going to be the best prank ever!

He only had Max left as a target. Mouse smirked as he took a bite of his apple. He slid a piece of cheese into his front pocket for Marty. Marty grabbed it with his green goo covered feet. But Mouse was too busy smiling to notice the goo covered feet as Marty munched away at the cheese.

But before he went after Max, he wanted to watch Rebekah's reaction to her missing history book. He knew that was her next class. When lunch was over he headed for her locker so that he could see what she thought of the green goo.

Rebekah opened her locker and reached inside for her history book. She knew she had left it on the top shelf so that she would be able to find it easily. She only had a few minutes between classes.

When she reached for it on the top shelf, there was nothing there. Well not just nothing, there was a horrible slime.

"Ugh!" she cried out as she drew her hand back. The slime was green and slippery. "Gross!"

"What's wrong Rebekah?" Mouse asked as he walked up beside her. He was trying very hard not to smile.

"My history book is missing," she growled and showed him her hand. "All that's left behind is this."

"Ew," he scrunched up his nose and reached into his backpack. He pulled out a tissue and handed it to her so that she could clean her hand. "Are you sure your history book is gone?" he asked. "Maybe you left it somewhere."

"I know I left it right there on the top shelf," Rebekah said sternly. "Even if I did misplace it, that doesn't explain the slime, now does it?"

She narrowed her eyes and glared at her locker. "I'm going to figure this out," she said with determination.

Mouse smirked a little but nodded. Just then the bell rang and Rebekah sighed.

"Great, now I'm going to be late and unprepared," she sighed as she hurried off down the hallway.

When she reached her history class and stepped inside, she spotted her history book. It was sitting right on her desk. "Weird!" she said as she picked up the book.

She watched as Mouse walked past the classroom door with a quick wave. Rebekah didn't know how her history book had gotten to her classroom without her, or why there was green goo in her locker, but she was glad that she had it back in time for class.

FIVE

Max was in science class, his favorite class of the day. Mouse could see him through the window from outside of the school. Mouse had gym for his last class of the day and they were running the field behind the school.

He slipped away around the second lap so he could sneak up on Max. Max was wearing thick safety goggles and gloves as he worked on his project. The teacher was walking between each of the desks watching closely.

Mouse spotted his target. It was Max's laboratory notebook. It kept a record of all of his experiments and results. He always had it with him.

Mouse picked up a clump of grass and tossed it at the window. It made a soft sound when it hit the window, but it was loud enough to get Max's attention. Max looked up with surprise toward the window. Mouse threw another clump of grass at the window.

"Mr. Bell look at this," Max called out as he walked toward the window. Mr. Bell and the other students in the class went over to the window to see what was going on. Mouse threw a few more clumps of grass toward the window.

"How strange," Mr. Bell said. "This sounds like the perfect thing to investigate. Why don't we all step outside and take a look? Any theories?" he asked as he led the students out of the classroom.

Mouse opened the window as soon as they were all out of the classroom. He jumped into the room and closed the window behind him. He reached into Max's bag and grabbed his laboratory notebook.

Marty slipped out of his pocket as he did.

"Oops," Mouse mumbled and reached into Max's bag to grab his pet. Then he squirted a bit of green goo on to the zipper of Max's bag.

He hurried out of the classroom with Max's notebook before the students could return.

When Max got back to his desk after finding nothing of interest outside, he returned to his experiment. He reached for his notebook to make a note, but it wasn't on the desk. He looked in his bag and didn't find it there either, but he did find green goo on his zipper.

"Ew," he muttered and used a paper towel to wipe it off. He looked all over the classroom for his notebook, but it was nowhere to be found.

SIX

Amanda was fuming by the time she reached her locker. She couldn't find her favorite glue anywhere. She was tucking her books away when she noticed something in the bottom of her book bag. It was the glue!

"How did it get here?" she asked with confusion. She knew she would never put it in the bottom of her bag. It could have squished out and gotten all over her books. "Strange," she shook her head, but she was glad to have it back. She set it carefully inside her locker and then rushed to catch her bus.

Jaden didn't want to leave school without his soccer ball. But he knew if he missed the bus it would be a long walk home. Some days he liked to walk, but today he was just too mad.

He wanted to get home and see if somehow his ball had magically appeared in his room. When he went to sit down in his usual seat on the bus, he almost sat on his soccer ball!

"How did this get here?" Jaden asked with surprise. He glanced around the bus, but none of the other kids seemed to know. He was happy to have it back, but he was still miffed that someone had taken it in the first place.

SEVEN

Rebekah called everyone after school. She had heard in passing about all of the things going missing and then being found. Being the detective that she was, she wanted to get to the bottom of it.

"I think we need to get together," she explained. "I think something strange is going on here."

All of her friends agreed. All except for Mouse of course.

"I think you're being a little too suspicious Rebekah," Mouse said with a laugh. "I'm sure that it's nothing."

"I don't call green goo in my locker nothing," Rebekah pointed out grimly.

"Alright, I'll be there," Mouse promised. He felt a little nervous agreeing to the meeting. Would they figure out that he had been the one behind it all?

He had a plan for the next day to show up at school in a ninja suit and really surprise them when he revealed that he was the one who played the prank. But if they figured it out before then, his prank would be ruined.

When he arrived at the tree house everyone was already there.

"Well at least we got everything back," Amanda was saying to Jaden as Mouse climbed up into the tree house.

"Got what back?" Mouse asked innocently as he sat down at the table with the rest of his friends.

"We all had something stolen from us today," Rebekah explained in a serious tone. "I had my history book taken, Jaden had his soccer ball taken, Amanda had her special glue stolen and Max had his notebook taken," Rebekah sighed and shook her head. "Didn't you have anything taken Mouse?" she asked.

"Now that you mention it," Mouse said quickly. "My lunch was missing today!" he didn't know what else to say, since he had to think of something quickly.

"Well I got my soccer ball back; it was on my seat on the bus!" Jaden said with a groan.

"My history book was in my history class," Rebekah frowned. "It doesn't make any sense. Why take something just to give it back?"

"I don't know but I was very happy when I found my glue in my bag," Amanda scrunched up her nose. "I could have done without the green goo though."

"Well you see, if you got everything back, then nothing was actually stolen," Mouse shrugged as if it was no big deal.

"Uh, hello?" Max waved his hand in the air. "I didn't get my notebook back and it means the world to me!"

Mouse's eyes widened as he realized that he had forgotten to put Max's notebook under his desk. He had been in such a rush to get Jaden's soccer ball on to his bus that he had forgotten all about Max's notebook. It was still in his backpack!

"Oh, I'm so sorry Max," Mouse said with a frown. Max nodded sadly.

"Sorry is not good enough," Rebekah announced sharply. Mouse winced, he was sure Rebekah had figured out it was him already. Luckily when she continued, it was clear that she hadn't figured it out.

"We need to find out who did this, get Max's notebook back and cover the criminal in green goo!" she said sternly.

"Well don't you think that's going a little far?" Mouse asked nervously.

"No!" Amanda piped up. "I got that goo in my hair Mouse," she pointed to her dark waves. "My hair!" she added in a high pitched voice.

"Oh," Mouse grimaced. "That does sound bad."

"And I for one don't like anyone sneaking into my locker," Rebekah said with a huff. "I have very important detective supplies in there."

"Not to mention that my soccer ball is like my best friend," Jaden pointed out. "Who knows what could have happened to it! What if I had walked home instead of taking the bus?"

Mouse frowned, he hadn't thought of that.

"And if I don't get my notebook back, all the hard work I've done all year is not going to matter! I have all my experiments and the results in there," Max hung his head. "I guess I should have been more careful with it."

Mouse actually felt bad for his friends. His joke wasn't working out to be as funny as he hoped. But he didn't want to tell them the truth. He had a better idea. He had yet another plan!

"Well listen guys, I'm sorry about all this. But since I didn't get my lunch back, I'm starving. Could we talk about this more tomorrow?" he asked hopefully.

"Alright I guess," Rebekah said with pursed lips.

"Tomorrow," Jaden nodded.

"How am I supposed to make it until tomorrow without my notebook?" Max moaned.

"Don't worry Max, maybe you'll get it back before then," Mouse suggested. Then he hurried out of the tree house.

EIGHT

He ran all the way home. He changed into the ninja suit he was saving for the next day. He grabbed Max's notebook and started to run back out of the house, when his mother called out to him.

"Mouse, my little ninja, where are you going?"

Mouse froze, and groaned under his breath. What kind of ninja was he if he couldn't even sneak past his mother?

"Just going out for a bit Mom," Mouse called over his shoulder.

"No you're not young man," she said sternly. Mouse's eyes widened as he wondered if he was in trouble for something.

"Not without the trash," she reminded him.

"Oh, sorry," Mouse said quickly. He hurried into the kitchen, grabbed the trash, and dropped it in the trash can.

His neighbor across the street was putting his trash out too. He stared strangely at Mouse in his ninja suit. Mouse waved to him and then ran down the street toward Max's house.

He was hoping that Max would still be at the tree house. When he reached Max's house he saw his mother's car in the driveway. He also saw that the trash can was still empty. He ducked down behind the bushes as Max's mother carried the trash out through the front door. As he hoped, she left the door open.

Mouse dashed into the house and up the stairs to Max's room. He dropped Max's notebook right down in the middle of his desk. Then he spun around to run in the other direction. When he did he nearly ran right into Max who was walking backwards into his room.

"I'm sorry Mom, I'll remember the trash next time, I promise!" he was calling out. Mouse dove under Max's bed. Max sighed and dropped his backpack on the floor. He walked over to his desk and sat down. Then he gasped.

"My notebook! It's here!" he said happily. "Mouse was right!"

He picked up his phone and called Rebekah. "Guess what, my notebook was here when I got home!" he said cheerfully. "Yes you're right," he agreed with something Rebekah said. "Sure, good idea, come on over!" he said before hanging up.

Mouse grimaced. He knew that if Rebekah came over to Max's house he would be stuck under Max's bed for quite some time.

Even worse, Marty had wriggled his way out of Mouse's pocket under his ninja suit. The mouse crawled right up through the collar of his ninja suit, tickling him the whole way. Mouse had to cover his mouth to keep from giggling, which meant that he couldn't catch Marty.

He watched as the mouse scampered across Max's carpet, leaving green goo footprints behind.

"Max!" his mother called from downstairs. "Your friend is here!"

Mouse sighed with relief when Max walked out of his room to greet Rebekah.

Mouse slipped out from under the bed, snatched up Marty and ducked out of the room and into the bathroom. Once he heard Max and Rebekah go into Max's room, he slipped out of the bathroom.

He ran out the front door and closed it quietly behind him. He ran all the way home. By the time he got there, he was exhausted. But at least Max had gotten his notebook back.

NINE

He was so tired that he decided to lay down for a nap. He set Marty into the large cage of mice that he had on a table in his room. Then he tossed his ninja suit on the floor and flopped down on his bed. He was asleep within minutes.

When Mouse opened his eyes again it was already dark out. He could smell his dinner cooking. He sat up on his bed and rubbed his eyes. When he put his feet down on the floor, he felt something sticky under them.

"Huh?" he blinked and reached for his lamp to turn on the light. When he grabbed the chain to pull it, he found that it was sticky too. "Ew!" he gasped and turned the light on. His hand was covered in green goo and so were his feet! Standing in his room were four ninjas! At least that's what they looked like, all dressed in black, with black ski masks on their faces.

"I think we've caught ourselves a Mouse ninja!" one of them announced. Mouse recognized the voice. It was Jaden! Before he could say a word to defend himself they all revealed the water guns they had been hiding behind their backs. They sprayed the guns and out shot green goo! It sprayed all over Mouse from head to toe.

"Ah! Stop!" Mouse pleaded and tried to get under his blanket.

"That's what you get Mouse ninja!" Rebekah hollered as she took off her mask. "It's not funny to play pranks on your friends!" she said and put her hands on her hips.

"Well it was a little funny," Amanda admitted as she pulled her mask off. Mouse was trying to wipe the goo off of his face.

"And now it's really funny," Max laughed as he pulled off his mask.

Jaden was laughing too when he pulled off his mask. "Good thing Rebekah figured it out!"

"Of course she did," Mouse groaned. "But how?"

"Your little mouse left footprints behind," Rebekah laughed. "We found tiny footprints and knew it had to be you. Plus, you didn't have anything stolen. Then after Max said he hadn't gotten his notebook back, you took off and suddenly it was back! Then of course there were more little mouse footprints."

"Oh and this confirmed it," Amanda added as she picked up his ninja suit off the floor.

"Plus your neighbor was ranting about ninjas and trash when we walked up," Jaden pointed out with a raised eyebrow. "I think he's a little freaked out."

"Heh, oops," Mouse grinned. "But you have to admit it was the best prank ever-" he started to say. He couldn't finish because his friends aimed their water guns and covered him in green goo again!

ALSO BY PJ RYAN

PJRyanBooks.com

* Sign up for my newsletter and get a
FREE Rebekah - Girl Detective e-book.

Rebekah - Girl Detective

Rebekah - Girl Detective Goes to Summer Camp

Rebekah - Girl Detective Fifth Grade Mysteries

Mouse's Secret Club

RJ - Boy Detective

Rebekah, Mouse & RJ: Special Editions

Jack's Big Secret

The Mermaids of Eldoris

The Fairies of Sunflower Grove

The Magic of Faylea

JOURNALS, PUZZLE BOOKS & MORE FUN

CPSIA information can be obtained
at www.ICGtesting.com
Printed in the USA
BVHW041651170223
658754BV00013B/418